Dangers of a FORGOTTEN PAST

Dangers of a FORGOTTEN PAST

MICHAEL HAYDEN

ARPress
ILLUMINATING IDEAS,
EMPOWERING VOICES

ARPress
45 Dan Road Suite 5
Canton MA 02021

Hotline: 1(800) 220-7660
Fax: 1(855) 752-6001

Ordering Information:
Quantity sales. Special discounts are available on quantity purchases by corporations, associations, and others. For details, contact the publisher at the address above.

Printed in the United States of America.

ISBN-13:   Paperback   979-8-89389-676-3
                eBook   979-8-89389-677-0

Library of Congress Control Number: 2024923818

Chapter 1

I f I had ever hoped to visit a universe where there was no life at all, I was definitely in the right place. I don't know how long I was there because I was nothing until it was time to leave. Life was returning like rekindling flames from sparks swirling from a gust of wind on smoldering coals of an abandoned campfire. And then I started to breathe.

I didn't know it yet, but seatbelts were holding me upside-down in a wrecked vehicle. I was in a predicament that very few would experience in a lifetime. It was the beginning of a long, arduous journey through an unforgettable nightmare.

As my senses slowly came to life, my body felt weightless and hovering eerily over a bottomless black hole. Random flashes of light occasionally darted in my head, coming from every direction. Sometimes, a scary distorted figure popped in and out of view like fireworks exploding in the night sky. Fear and anxiety flooded my brain and awoke intense pain as my senses returned. My entire world was spinning.

After a few chaotic moments, I started hearing faint but recognizable noises. It sounded like leaves dancing across stones, pushed by the wind whistling down through the trees above. The smell of dirt mixed with gasoline was almost overpowering, causing me to shiver in the cold, humid air.

As my mind cleared, I assumed an accident must have knocked me out. Unfortunately, my senses had brought severe pain dominating my thoughts. A hammer was pounding inside my swollen head. When I moved my head from side to side to examine the surrounding area the pain was almost unbearable and the spinning sensation got worse, causing nausea. The blurred vision in my swollen left eye was worsened by the burning sensation around it.

After blinking and shaking my head several times, the spinning subsided, but my eye felt like it had disappeared into the back of my head. I panicked as I helplessly dangled from the seatbelts realizing I had no idea how I had gotten there. Blood rushed to my head causing it to feel like it was going to explode. The speedometer and odometer on the dashboard were now visible to my good eye but I couldn't get a sense of my surroundings. To make matters worse, it was nighttime and the darkness made it hard to see.

I was terrified and trembling with fear, so I started breathing more slowly to calm myself down. After several deep breaths, I started squirming and twisting my body attempting to free myself. I couldn't move very much because the seatbelt had me tightly wedged against the dented door and the buckle was jammed. After several more futile attempts to unhook the seatbelt I looked around and spotted a long-pointed shard of glass broken from the rearview mirror, lying on the ceiling of the vehicle. When I stretched to pick it up, the pain snaked up my shoulders and neck causing me to shriek.

When I finally grabbed the glass, the sharp edges cut into my thumb and index finger, causing another involuntary groan.

Red drops of blood trickled down my fingers mirroring the tears rolling down my cheeks from the pain.

I dropped the glass and slid my bloody fingers into my mouth sucking on them until the bleeding nearly stopped. The mixture of blood and dirt was unpleasant and gritty in my mouth. When I rubbed my teeth together, the dirt felt like scratching a blackboard. It was hard to find enough saliva to wet the inside of my mouth to spit out the debris.

When I wiped the remaining blood from my hand on my shirt I whenced as some splinters of glass sunk deeper into my thumb, so I carefully removed them, one at a time. After tearing the bottom of my shirt, I wrapped it around one end of the shard of glass to protect my hand and carefully angled the sharp edge onto the seatbelt. With a sawing motion I could feel and hear it slowly ripping apart. After what seemed like an eternity, the glass sliced through the fabric with one final stroke. When the last strand tore apart, the seatbelt snapped, and I plopped down abruptly with a loud thud.

The impact was hard and took my breath away. "Ahhh, damn!" I cried.

The full weight of my body was on my shoulders pressing against the surface beneath me. My chin was tucked tightly against my chest with my feet up in the air, against the front seat. It was hard to breathe and I knew I had to get out of that position quickly to avoid suffocating. After twisting my body back and forth several times, I was finally able to straighten my neck and tilt my head backward, allowing me to breathe more freely.

After catching my breath, I slowly inched my way towards the shattered front passenger window and felt sure my body would fit through the narrowed opening. I was thankful that there were no other persons in the vehicle. All I had to do was worry about myself. But I was very frightened and all alone, and it was dark outside.

The bent window frame made it hard to wiggle through the opening but there was enough room. Twisting and turning were physically challenging and the sharp beads of broken glass scuffed my face and shoulder as I finally freed my body from the wreckage. Warmblood now smeared my face and neck and even though the wounds were superficial they were raw and painful.

When I laid next to the side view mirror, I saw my reflection but didn't recognize the person with the swollen left eye and an ugly purple bump on the top of his bloody head. At that moment, I realized that I couldn't remember my name either.

When I checked my body, I noticed that despite the ugly bruises on my arms and face there didn't seem to be any life-threatening injuries.

I looked again in the side view mirror. Dirt filled my bushy mustache and hid my upper lip. There were big patches of red welts on my shoulders and chest, and I knew they would eventually turn into ugly bruises. Bruises circled each of my wrists, and they felt numb, like there was nerve damage. It looked like my wrists had been bound tightly with a rope. When I straightened and flexed my hands and fingers, the pain shot through them like lightning bolts. They were stiff and numb, so I rubbed them together to restore circulation.

I bent my legs and flexed them up and down, relieved that nothing felt like it was broken or sprained.

I studied the bruises on my wrists again. "Had I been tied up? Was I kidnapped?"

My blue jeans were ripped on my right leg, exposing an abrasion on my calf. My shoulders were partly exposed from tears on my soiled burgundy polo shirt. I was wearing a brown pair of leather sandals that were severely scuffed and torn, exposing scratches and specks of blood on my toes. They were not the kind of footwear needed for mountainous terrain.

I couldn't find a watch or any other jewelry on my body. There was no cell phone, keys, or coins in any of my pockets.

Even though I was beaten up and sore, I could still move around. After scooting further away from the wreckage, my body was about three feet outside the window frame. Even though it smelled like gasoline had drained from the vehicle, the leaks had stopped, and the ground was dry.

After lying on my back for about a minute, I slowly rolled onto my side and took a deep breath. My head was throbbing, and my ribs were sore. Dizziness and nausea returned, so I waited until they subsided. For the first time, I felt cold raindrops intermittently pelting my face. Then I looked up noticed patches of grey clouds with openings exposing clusters of stars in the sky. It actually felt good but reminded me that I was very thirsty, so I opened my mouth, letting the droplets splash on my tongue to relieve the dryness, but it was just enough to worsen matters.

When I raised my head, I looked back at the wreckage. A dark green off-road vehicle appeared to have landed upside down in a sandy area beneath a ledge surrounded by pine trees. I was so disoriented; I plopped my head back onto the ground again, spreading my arms and legs, and stayed for several minutes, hoping to regain composure. At least the steady raindrops were starting to have a calming effect.

Finally, I struggled to a sitting position and shook my head. I rose slowly and staggered to my knees, continuing to check my surroundings. The ground was damp, but there were no puddles of water visible on the sand anywhere. I could hear and feel bigger and colder droplets splattering mud and, on my head, and arms.

The rocks beneath me were stabbing into my knees, so I kept shifting my weight back and forth. Finally, I struggled to a standing position. When I started walking, the stiffness in my back caused me to reach for the Jeep's tire to steady myself.

After circling the vehicle, I looked to the left of a green Jeep. It appeared to be an older Cherokee model. I assumed it was mine. It looked like it was a 1980's model with a rusted tailpipe. The paint was faded and rusted in several places like it had been left out in the elements for extended periods.

When I looked directly above the Jeep, I saw a steep embankment and was confident it led to a road from where the car must have rolled. A tall pine tree wasn't far, so I crawled to the base of it and rested against the rough bark. I closed my eyes and was greeted with a painful reminder of my injured left eye. I started slowly inhaling and exhaling so my body could relax. But I still felt vulnerable because I couldn't remember who I was, where I was coming from, or might have been going. But I also had a deep sense of gratitude that I was still alive, not seriously injured, and could walk. I rechecked my pockets, hoping that I missed something but was again disappointed to find them empty.

"My wallet must have fallen out during the rollover," I thought.

After several minutes I decided to go back to the Jeep to check again to see what I could find. There had to be a vehicle registration in the glove compartment, and it would tell me who I was and give my address. I stood up with a loud grunt but had to brace myself against a pine tree.

I shook my head vigorously again, trying to get rid of the cobwebs. But it was a mistake because it triggered a violent attack of vertigo, and I stumbled to the ground. After catching my breath, I grabbed the tree trunk and groaned as my hands pulled my battered frame up the bark until my entire body was steady against it.

I staggered to the Jeep, got down on my hands and knees, and put my arm around the right front tire to brace myself. The blood on my face and shoulder was dry, and the wounds burned like road rash. I brushed some of the dirt off with my hands before reaching inside.

Inside, I opened the glove compartment and was disappointed that neither the registration nor insurance paperwork was there. Nothing was there. After crouching to my hands and knees again, I crawled around the vehicle. I looked everywhere in and around the Jeep and was unable to find anything at all. Except for the broken glass inside the car, it was surprisingly clean, and there were no belongs there, not even a piece of paper. It didn't seem to add up and was discouraging.

Since it was already dark, I struggled up the embankment, stopping every few seconds to ease the pain in my legs, hips, and back. I rested a few minutes at a time to catch my breath. Once I got to the top of the ledge above the wreckage, I discovered a not-so-well maintained gravel road that had deep tire tracks crisscrossing in every direction. When I looked back down the embankment from the road, I couldn't see the Jeep anymore because the jagged sandstone ledge was jutting out in front of me and obstructing it. I had to take about fifteen steps back down the road before seeing the back end of the Jeep.

I estimated that I was somewhere in a mountainous area, possibly in the western part of the United States. I was thirsty, without water, discouraged, and scared. Panic had again taken over, so I closed my eyes and clenched my fist, determined to regain self-control. Several deep breaths calmed my nerves enough to keep going. I desperately tried to remember why and how I got here, but still, nothing looked familiar. After a few minutes, the fog had almost completely cleared from my head, and I felt more in control.

Since I was sure the road had to end up somewhere populated, I decided to walk down from the higher terrain. Hopefully, it would eventually lead me out of the mountains. But nothing was certain. The road had a rocky and curvy decline, and it was challenging to navigate in my current disoriented condition. But for now, I was hoping that going down rather than up was the best direction.

Before leaving, I searched the entire area again, including the Jeep, to see if I could find my wallet or any other potential identifiers but was again unsuccessful. I got down on my hands and knees again and searched one last time inside the Jeep. Nothing was there.

Because of the periodic dizziness, I was concerned that I had had a concussion or worse, so I knew I had to be careful hiking down the rugged path. As I staggered and stumbled further and further down the road, I became increasingly discouraged and was exhausted. It seemed like I had been walking for over an hour and had seen nothing familiar. The rain drizzled for a while but eventually stopped.

By now, I was able to resist throwing up despite nausea. I experienced some confusion too, but thirst and cottonmouth were starting to dominate my thoughts. I worried about my physical endurance too.

"What if I have a fractured skull? What if I have bleeding inside my brain? Am I going to die up here?"

I sat and leaned forward, lost my balance momentarily, and then threw up violently. A taste of bile and acid erupted from my stomach, and it caused me to throw up again, with some of it coming out my nose. I struggled to stop the urge to throw up. Slow breathing finally allowed my system to calm down enough for my body to relax. The pounding in my head gradually lessened as well.

The surrounding darkness and the unknown added to my anxiety. It was my worst obstacle. And what about me?

"Was I a criminal on the run or an innocent victim? Did I have any friends who would notice I was missing and start looking for me?"

Suddenly, I felt so exhausted that I slumped on a big rock with my back against a pine tree next to the road. My head started spinning again, and everything went black. At least, the fear and pain were gone for the moment, and there were no dreams or nightmares, only darkness.

And there were no questions about me, for now.

Chapter 2

The sunbeams forced my eyes to open as they filtered through the trees. I felt warmth replacing the cold that had stiffened the skin on my face. As the brightness increased, it was harder to keep my eyes open. I squinted while shading them with my open hand just above my eyebrows. When I stretched my body, I heard bones crackling, causing me to moan. I thought about the painful memories of how I got from the wreckage to this spot. My back had slid off the tree while I was asleep and had left me flat on my back, causing sharp, crumbled glass to sink into the skin on my back. It felt like I had dents in my back. As I struggled to a sitting position, I started to gag, but nothing came out. My head was spinning again, and the pain was throbbing inside my skull.

I kept shifting my position back and forth to relieve some of the pain. But then, I lost my balance and rolled down onto my left side causing me to dry heave again. There was nothing left in my stomach to throw up. I pulled myself up to a sitting position again and wiped some remnants of bitter-tasting bile from onto my hands. It stunk like soured decay. I wiped it on my torn pants, but the foul odor was still strong. I was lying in an awkward position on the rocky terrain for hours, causing stiffness in every part of my body. I started moving my arms and legs again to make sure there were no broken bones. Aside from the aches and pains, I was relieved that my bones felt undamaged.

"Where am I?"

"Who the hell am I?"

It was very discouraging, and the fear was overwhelming. My mouth was so dry I could hardly swallow. My lips were chapped so that when I moved them, they felt like painful paper cuts.

My surroundings were still totally unfamiliar, and I had only a general sense of time, thanks to the sun's daylight and position. I started inhaling and exhaling slowly and closed my eyes in an attempt to get some control over my emotions and fear. Even that movement was painful.

At least it wasn't dark anymore, making me feel less afraid. I could see the trees, rocks, and sand around me, and for a brief moment, I was overwhelmed by the beauty of it all.

After a few more minutes, my head began to settle, and the spinning subsided. I struggled to stay focused and checked my surroundings more closely. Nothing I saw or heard provided encouraging clues about where I might be. I was keenly aware of my defenseless situation, so I searched until I found a thick and straight tree branch about the length of a baseball bat. The shape of one end was without bark, and the smooth surface was easier to grip. The broken branches and rough bark on the other end would prove to be painful if it struck an intruder.

As I moved very slowly downhill, my joints loosened up, and some of the soreness became more tolerable. Having no water was a big problem, and I had little protection from the sweltering sun. I was going to have to find a populated area soon. It made it impossible to relax. I frequently hallucinated images of tiny creatures moving through the trees and underbrush. I worried about coyotes, bears, or even mountain lions that might be in the area. I was so frightened that it was hard to think of anything else. I reacted to every sound or movement around me and purposely stopped occasionally breathing to hear better and being lost with no memory magnified the fear and feelings of hopelessness. It took everything I had to fight off the panic. The only thing I felt confident about was that going downhill probably made more sense than going uphill.

After what felt like an eternity, the sun had crept up almost directly overhead, so it was around noon. I was able to determine that I was going northwest, based on the direction of the sun and the moss on the north side of the trees. But that had very little meaning because I had no idea where my route was taking me. I didn't know if I was getting closer or further away from civilization.

My lips were peeling and painful as they continued to split open, and I could hardly swallow. I was exhausted and aching all over and wondered if I could continue much further without dying from exposure. My obvious choice was to keep walking as long as I could. Even though my steps had been slow and labored initially, they had significantly quickened despite the fatigue, and I was afraid to stop. In the beginning, it had been hard to keep my balance, and occasionally I stumbled. But the fog in my head had cleared, and I was able to walk without staggering. My attention continued to be focused on finding landscapes that would discover signs of human life. All I could do is hope my choices would lead to the rescue.

My thoughts were interrupted because I hadn't looked at the license plate on the back of the Jeep. Had I done so I might have gotten some important clues about where I was. It was too late and too far to turn back, and the pain from bruises on my wrists reminded me that I might still be in some danger. Now my wrists looked like I was wearing reddish-purple bracelets.

"I had to have been tied up," I thought.

After almost two hours of a steady pace, I sat down and rested next to a cedar tree that shaded me from the sun. The terrain had changed dramatically from jagged rocks to sandy foothills, low-lying brush, cedar, and piñon trees. I could see at a greater distance now, including clearings that exposed a lot of blue skies. My body was exhausted now, and I was starting to feel very weak. My thirst was magnified by the knowledge that I had no water. But now, I was beginning to understand how strong my survival instincts were. I was also afraid that if I stopped for very long, I might give up. I was determined to keep going until there was nothing left to give.

My mind kept wandering, but nothing emerged about my past. The more I tried to remember, the greater the anxiety and frustration grew. My skin was turning bright pink, and I had no cover. It caused a burning sensation, and there was nothing I could do about it for now, so, I tried to ignore it.

Birds were singing around me, forcing a smile. There were so many, and they genuinely sounded musical.

"How could they be so happy when I was in so much danger," I wondered as I caught a glimpse of a roadrunner darting across the hot sand right in front of me. It stopped and studied me as if I was an invader in his world. He seemed fearless. Then, just as quickly, he darted away, disappearing into the surrounding Chamisa bushes.

After several minutes of walking, I was startled by a rattling sound to my left, just a few feet away. When I turned and looked in that direction, my eyes widened and quickly focused on a sandy-colored rattlesnake with dark brown diamond markings and about 2-3 feet long with darker colored diamond shapes on his back. It was just about ten feet to the right of me. He wasn't coiled but hissed, and his tongue kept darting in and out with a menacing rhythm as he stared in my direction. It had caught me by surprise, but I quietly backed away until I was at a safe distance while he slinked away from view, but I could still see his movements in the weeds. I quietly walked in the opposite direction looking back frequently to make sure he wasn't close by. At that time, I was pretty sure it was a diamondback rattlesnake and poisonous.

I trudged down the rocky hill at a quicker pace for about 25 yards. But now, I found myself constantly looking around, expecting another snake to appear. The snake took so much of my attention that the faint familiar sounds beyond the foothills went unnoticed. I was excited because it sounded like wheels humming rapidly over the pavement. I steadied myself against a short-gnarly cedar and rested while I summoned the strength to stretch up, standing on my toes trying to look over the hill that was blocking my vision. I guessed that I was somewhere in the southwestern part of the U.S., and it seemed strangely familiar. Knowing this presented some fragmented memories.

After taking a few deep breaths, I continued to struggle over the sand and boulders. The more I walked, the louder the sounds became, causing more excitement.

A few minutes later, I came to an opening and was overcome with relief to see a four-lane highway about 100 yards away. A few cars quickly passed as I approached. As I neared the highway's shoulder, I was a little frustrated because I couldn't see any road signs at first. Eventually, my good eye captured a white sign with black letters that read NM 333. I could hear and see another more prominent highway in the distance on the other side of the road. There was a lot of noisier traffic, and it had six lanes. I crossed NM 333 and kept walking until I saw a red, white, and blue I-40 sign on the side. After stepping onto the shoulder of the road, I looked both ways several times. Based on the sun, I realized the traffic on this side of the road was heading east.

It was sweltering by now, and I noticed that the skin on my arms was a bright red. It felt like my skin was cooking. I started worrying about having a sunstroke. Sweat was rolling down my face and into my eyes. My lips were severely cracked, and they hurt when I tried to close my mouth. I hadn't drunk any water for several hours, and my tongue was sticking to the roof of my mouth. After chewing the dry skin on my lower lip, and I could taste blood trickling onto the tip of my tongue, and it seemed to dry almost immediately on my tongue.

More off-road vehicle traffic was visible and moving quickly in both directions. The hum of the tires intensified as semi's rushed past, and the gust of wind they produced shoved me back. I stuck my thumb up in the air as traffic approached. A few vehicles sped past, but the passengers never looked at me as though I was invisible.

I was confused about why I could remember some basic things but nothing about me or my past. That made me insecure and afraid. By now, my headache had lessened, but sunburn had replaced that pain. I needed to get out of the sun as quickly as possible. But what I needed most was water and first aid.

My hopes began to sink as one vehicle after the other sped by without even slowing down. At least ten more minutes had passed, and now my skin was bright red.

"Maybe this was all a dream, and none of it is really happening," I thought.

"What a relief it would be to just wake up."

But it wasn't a dream. It seemed like a nightmare.

Suddenly, a bicyclist emerged at the top of the hill on the west horizon and raced towards me. As the bicyclist got closer, I frantically stood in his way and waved my arms in the air. I tried to yell for help, but my throat was so dry there was only a whispering sound.

The bicyclist appeared to be a man in his early thirties and was in good physical condition. He had a lean physique covered with skin-tight red and black bicycler attire and a helmet matching his unruly red hair and mustache. He was wearing BMW sports shoes with red ankle socks. As he got closer, he slowed to a stop and removed the earbuds that were attached to his cell phone tucked neatly into an armband. As the bicyclist studied me, I could see a suspicious expression on his face. But it quickly changed when he got closer and saw my bloody and sunburned face. I promptly attempted to look as non-threatening as possible by dropping the branch I had been carrying and showing the palms of my hands.

"I need help!"

My voice was very raspy, so the bicycler leaned forward to hear better. But he did not doubt that I was in terrible condition. He continued to study me as he straddled the seat of his bicycle and with his feet squarely on the gravel.

"What's going on?" he asked.

I pointed up the side of the mountain in the direction of the paved road. "I had a car accident up there. My car rolled and is still up there. I need help and have a head injury. I can't remember anything, and I'm dying of thirst. I don't even know who I am. I think I have a concussion because I was unconscious for a long time."

The bicyclist showed some concern as he backed away. He pulled out the cell phone from his armband and dialed 911. When he got a response on the other end, he shared the information provided by me and gave our location to the dispatcher. He then told me I was near the town of Tijeras in the Sandia mountains, close to Albuquerque, New Mexico.

The bicyclist quickly handed me his water bottle and then asked, "Can you remember anything about how you got here?" He asked with a strong southern accent.

After drinking almost all the water from his bottle, I said. "Sorry, man, my apologies. I'm dehydrated."

"No problem," he answered. He then handed me his other bottle. "Go ahead and drink all you want. You need it more than I do."

"I can't remember anything at all about me right now. You said we were in the Sandia Mountains in Albuquerque. That sounds familiar, but nothing more. How close are we to Albuquerque?"

"We're about a dozen miles from there. You must have lost control of your vehicle on an off-road trail up there. It can be pretty rugged and dangerous if you don't know where you're going. I'm sure you're disoriented. Were you drinking?"

I shrugged my shoulders. "I don't think so."

"I'll wait here with you until an ambulance arrives."

The bicyclist reached for the third bottle of water from a saddlebag behind his seat.

"No, thank you. You need some too."

"Not as bad as you do. Take it!"

"My name is Rick Sanders, said the bicyclist. "I am from Edgewood and I am training for a cross country cycling competition."

"I nodded as I drank the rest of the second bottle of water.

"What day is this?"

"Friday, June third, 2019."

After thinking about it for a few moments, I realized that it wasn't much help for my memory. But I was feeling much safer now and had noticeably calmed down.

We sat on some huge rocks close enough to the highway to be easily seen. Rick was kind enough to hand a Clif Energy Bar to me from his fanny pack. Then he passed his helmet to me and said, "You need this to wear as cover from the sun. I'll take it back when the ambulance gets here."

It wasn't until I tore the wrapper and took a bite that I realized how starved I was. I wolfed it down in less than a minute. We spent most of the remaining time talking about how I got down from my wreck. I was still hoarse and had to force the words out. The energy bar didn't cause me to start throwing up again, so I was relieved. It settled me down, and I felt some life coming back to my body.

About fifteen minutes later, I heard faint sounds of sirens from down the road. An Albuquerque Rescue vehicle was followed by a Fire Truck and Bernalillo County Sheriff's Unit. As they got louder, I was overcome by an incredible sense of relief and gratitude.

A young, stocky EMT wearing a black uniform and EMS Body Armor laid me on a gurney and loaded me into the Rescue vehicle after inserting an IV. He was a Hispanic male somewhere in his 40's, had a disproportionate waistline and big forearms. In a monotonous tone, he checked my vitals while questioning me about my accident. My responses were not much help. I couldn't even give a license plate number since I had failed to check, and with no Id, I was a mystery to all of us.

The younger of the two BCSO officers looked like he was a new officer in his early 20's with big shoulders and a slim waistline. His facial expressions were stern as he kept asking me if I had been drinking alcohol or if I was on any drugs. All I could say is that I didn't think so. He gave me a breathalyzer test, and alcohol was undetectable. I knew that blood would be drawn and sent to the lab from the hospital after getting a warrant to see if I was under the influence of drugs. I also figured if it turned up positive, I might be spending some time in jail. But I was also curious about whether there were any drugs in my system. I consented to the blood test.

Initially, the older officer informed me that they would have to leave on another call and might not be able to recover the vehicle until the following day. He was in his late 40's to early '50s. His short hair was mostly grey, and he had a large waistline stretching his tan shirt and pants outward. His face was wrinkled, and his forehead was jutting out over deep-set blue eyes. He confirmed that, depending on the blood test results, I might be looking at a stay in jail. His confirmation unnerved me. The EMT saw the fright in my eyes and said,

"Don't worry about that now. Let's get you stabilized."

Before the officers could leave, I asked them to look at the bruises on my wrist.

"I think I was a victim of foul play here," I told them.

Both officers examined the bruises, and the older-looking officer nodded. He said, "It looks like you were tied up alright. We need to find the vehicle ASAP!" He dispatched for another Unit with directions based on what I had provided. The younger officer agreed to wait to aid in the search.

The ambulance had to drive further east before they could cross the freeway to make a U-turn towards the west. The emergency responders transported me to the UNM hospital in Albuquerque. Upon arrival, I was given some routine tests, and the ER Dr. informed me that aside from multiple bruises and a concussion, it didn't appear too serious, but I needed to stay there for observation.

"Please tell me there are no drugs or alcohol in my system," I thought.

The physician was wearing a white coat and carrying a clipboard with a form. He was a young dark-skinned African American man in his early 40's with short graying hair and round brown plastic-framed glasses. He introduced himself as Dr. Calvin Lewis while reviewing my chart and asked more questions about my predicament. I couldn't answer any of the parts regarding me, the person. He said they were still waiting for the results of my blood tests but would let me know when they were available.

Even though he didn't have to, Dr. Lewis reminded me how lucky I was to have avoided more serious injuries. My skull had no fractures, and there was no evidence of bleeding in the brain. But there was a golf ball-sized bump on the top of my head. One of my wrists was sprained, and it felt like there was some nerve damage because it tingled, and the feeling in my fingers hadn't completely returned.

The Dr. then told me that once released, I would need to abstain from alcohol or any drugs because it could cause complications for the concussion. He then said he saw no symptoms to prescribe medications. He recommended Tylenol for the aches and pains.

"You also have amnesia," he added. "It isn't uncommon to have amnesia after a head injury like yours. Your memory will probably return completely. How long it will take is unpredictable," he speculated. "For some, it comes back pretty quickly. Others it comes back a little bit at a time and for others all at once. I know it's probably pretty frightening for you right now, but we'll help you through it," he added.

The doctor decided to keep me overnight for observation and hoped that I would remember a relative or friend to help me obtain my personal information so I would have a place to go once released. Of course, my most pressing fear was if there were drugs in my system. If not, once the vehicle is found and they investigate the license plate number, they might trace my identity.

It was nice to be in the hospital in a comfortable bed, but I was constantly awakened throughout the night, being checked by medical staff. Even though I felt safe, I already thought it would be nice to get out of there.

Later that morning, I was relieved to learn that the test confirmed no alcohol in my system, but there were other concerns about what was in my blood. The negative results for alcohol meant a lot, but now I was worried about drugs in my system and what that would mean. Dr. Lewis told me that he would be back to discuss it when BSCO officers arrived to obtain the report, and then he could review it with us. But I insisted he tell me right away. He said I had enough Ketamine to have potentially kill me.

"Ketamine? What the hell is that?"

"It's a date rape drug but is used for other purposes. Some law enforcement officers use it to subdue suspects during an arrest."

None of the information was helpful to me. It just caused more fear and anxiety.

Before law enforcement could read the results, I had to give consent. If I didn't, they would get a warrant anyway, so I might as well give it.

Now I wondered if I would be arrested for driving under the influence of drugs and was it because of a reckless night of partying or a symptom of something much bigger.

Chapter 3

The following day a BCSO officer visited me. He introduced himself as Officer Jim Taylor. He had short dark brown hair and brown eyes. He was about 6' tall and very fit. His hair was typical, with the sides sheared to the skin and the top about an inch long. He was wearing a Kevlar vest under his shirt and was armed with a Glock holstered to his side. He would have looked very intimidating had he not had a broad, engaging grin on his face. He asked, "Do you feel like answering some questions?"

"Yes, I'll answer any questions you have."

Officer Taylor asked me if I was sure about the location of the accident because he and another officer couldn't find his vehicle with the directions I had given. After I went through the directions again, Officer Taylor shook his head, confirming his previous conclusion.

"There was no vehicle in that location. We saw many tire tracks going in both directions on the trail, but there was no vehicle. Are you sure about where it happened? You could be confused from the head injury."

I shook my head, "That is all I remember...I hope I remembered. Now I'm not sure anymore,"

"It's okay, Officer Taylor answered. "You had a concussion and other problems that may have affected your memory. Do you remember anything more than what you told me initially?"

"I have been racking my brain, and I'm so frustrated! I can't remember anything!"

The officer's expression changed to a more serious one as he asked, "Do you know what Ketamine is?"

I frowned and then answered, "I had never heard of it until Dr. Lewis told me it was a date rape drug, and you guys sometimes use it to subdue suspects."

"When we tested your blood for alcohol and drugs, you had no alcohol, but must have had dangerously high concentrations of ketamine, which is, as you said, a date rape drug. It was probably so high you're lucky to be alive. Does that information mean anything at all?"

I thought for a moment and then shook my head and started to panic. I looked around and was stunned. I shook my head again and answered, "Nothing! Nothing at all! What the hell...?"

Officer Taylor then reassured me, "This is an open investigation. You are being treated as a victim and not a suspect for anything right now. You have bruises on your wrists, which strongly suggests your hands were tied. Either you lost consciousness with the drug while driving, which is highly unlikely because the drug usually acts so quickly, or someone tried to make it look like an accident. If that's the case, they made a mistake because they should have disconnected the seatbelts first. You would have probably been thrown from the vehicle and killed. But we need to find your car. Think about the location more and let me know if you remember anything. Maybe when you get released from the hospital, you can go up with me to the site of the wreck to see if we can locate it, okay?"

"Of course," I said, but my mind was turning summersaults over the new information. Ketamine was a drug I hadn't heard of before. In my current state of mind, I couldn't imagine taking it knowingly.

Taylor then asked, "Would you be willing to have your fingerprints taken and give a DNA sample? That might help us identify you and match you to a close relative."

"Of course, Officer."

At that moment, a sudden rush of fear went through my whole body. Maybe I was involved in a terrible crime. Maybe my mind didn't want to recall it.

Officer Taylor removed a DNA kit from his pocket and swabbed my mouth.

"This should take about a week if we're lucky." When you come to the office, I'll take your prints."

"Okay, thanks," I said. Then, for a brief instance, I wondered if I might be a criminal who double-crossed my partners and was trying to escape from them. Maybe I was okay with being that type of person. The thought was chilling. It made me even more anxious. Now I was unsure whether I wanted to know who I was.

Officer Taylor had noticed my reaction and said, "Don't worry about it for now. If you worry about it, it might make it harder for you to remember anything. Just be thankful you're alive. As I said, once you get released, maybe we can go up to where you think you were, and it might jog your memory so we can find the actual location of your vehicle. If we can find it, I believe we'll have a better chance of recovering your identity. Do you happen to remember anything that was on the license plate?"

"I wish I could, officer. I never looked there. I was so damned disoriented. I can't believe I didn't think of it."

Officer Taylor smiled and gave me his card as he walked towards the corridor. After going through the door into the hall, he peeked back in the room and repeated, "Don't worry about it for now. The most important thing is for you to get better so we can find your vehicle to move forward in our investigation. We have also put out a nationwide alert for missing persons with your photo. I bet that you're from Albuquerque or nearby. We might hear something pretty quick. Either way, we'll take it step-by-step."

I nodded and answered, "I would be encouraged to find a friend or anyone who knows me. It would speed things up for my memory."

"Get some rest, and I'll see you soon," Officer Taylor added. "Don't forget to call when you get released."

He looked inside the door again and asked, "By the way, what would you like for me to call you?"

At first, I shrugged my shoulders and shook my head cluelessly, but after a few moments, I smiled, "Call me Guy. That should make it easy for everyone to remember."

Officer Taylor returned my smile, "Okay, that works for me. It sounds like you might have been a comedian in a past life. I'll talk to you later, Guy." We both laughed as he left down the corridor to the elevator.

I had no place to go. I didn't have any clue about who to contact or where even to begin. One of the nurses told me that the hospital was already working on some placement and support system.

After settling into the chair next to my bed, I picked up an Albuquerque Journal left in my room on my tray. I glanced at the headlines while I stretched, checking to see how sore I was. Everything hurt. As I thumbed through the pages, I saw a small article under the Metro section that made my eyes widen. It reported, "Wandering man in Tijeras Canyon found." The story was brief but accurate, including a reference to my amnesia. It also appealed to anyone who might know me to come forward. The BCSO telephone contact number was at the end of the article. But it occurred to me that it might also be giving information to anyone who sought to find and hurt me.

At about 11:00 am, a social worker, Carolyn Maestas, visited me. She was wearing a white blouse and knee-length black skirt with black stockings and comfortable walking shoes. She was petite, in her mid-forties and about 5' tall. Her medium-length satin black hair, dark brown eyes, and contoured eyebrows complimented her attractive smile. Her black plastic framed glasses matched her hair and gave her a professional appearance. She appeared very fit, giving me the impression that she was a disciplined person. I could feel her energy too. She began the interview by assuring me that the hospital would have a placement for me, and it would be a safe place to go while I recovered from the accident. She scribbled several notes on her clipboard throughout the interview. After asking the required additional personal questions that

I couldn't answer, she recommended a temporary bed at a local Shelter. She seemed sincerely concerned for my welfare.

Since I couldn't identify any relatives or friends there weren't any alternatives for the shelter bed. I had no address or identity. She recommended the Albuquerque Shelter Center (ASC) for a short-term stay and seemed very optimistic that my memory would return sooner than later and would speed up a return me to everyday life. It made no sense to establish a long-term plan for now. I told her that I was going by the name of "Guy" for the time being. She laughed and shrugged her shoulders. After a few seconds, she laughed again.

"Well, that's original," she quipped.

Her laugh momentarily changed the atmosphere to a more personal setting.

When she asked that I sign some of the forms, we agreed that I would sign "Guy Unknown." That was fine with me. I was making some progress. Now I started to get a sense of direction and felt that there were people I could trust to help me recover. But I was still struggling to recall the traumatic events in the mountains. It seemed that someone might have tried to kill me, and in a violent way. I kept wondering what I had done to cause it. If someone wanted to kill me, he or they might be looking for me right now. At the very least, my injuries were consistent with violence against me. For now, I had no reference point to find out why. Maybe Officer Taylor was thinking the same thing. Would he turn from advocate to enforcer? The more I thought about it, I could feel the knots tightening in my stomach and the anxiety it brought. I had to find out more, and I couldn't do that without regaining some memory, and I couldn't do it from a hospital bed.

Carolyn Maestas had been watching me and detected the apprehension. She put the paperwork on the edge of my hospital bed and said, "It won't help anything to worry. I know that's easier said than done, but you have to trust the professionals working with you. We all want what's best and will make sure you don't have to go through this alone.

I thanked her before she left, but her reassurances weren't helpful. I knew I couldn't get better until I started remembering things.

Chapter 4

Dr. Lewis gave me a release time of 1:00 pm from the hospital, so I called Officer Taylor from the number on his agency card. Taylor agreed to provide me with a ride to the shelter after fingerprinting. Then we would schedule a visit to the mountains to find my Jeep depending on my condition. While getting my prints, Taylor studied my hands. He noticed that my eyes were on him, so he smiled and said,

"From looking at your smooth hands, I think you didn't work in a labor job. They're soft, and I don't see any callouses."

At first, I felt defensive about his remark, but he was right, so I shrugged my shoulders and joked, "Maybe I'm just a genius, Officer Taylor smiled, "Yep, that must be it. But your brilliance couldn't have involved driving skills."

"Maybe not, but it's hard to drive with your hands tied."

"I agree. And it's crucial to find out why and who was driving."

Officer Taylor was right. If I can't remember that information, I could be like a sitting duck right now. Someone could do just about anything, and I wouldn't see it coming.

The bump on my head was much smaller now, and the swelling around my eye was almost gone. The skin was a yellowish-purple color.

I had two black eyes. The Dr. had finally prescribed Tylenol for the pain, but I wasn't taking them now. The ache had been replaced with a soreness.

Officer Taylor arrived to pick me up right at 1:00 pm.

"How are you, Guy?"

"I feel better and am in a lot less pain."

Officer Taylor then asked me if I could handle a ride to the mountains. I hesitated at first but agreed because I was anxious to see the license plate on the Jeep and to see if it would help bring back any memories.

During the ride through Albuquerque on east I-40, we talked about how important it would be to find the Jeep. When we finally got to the road off the highway leading up to the rugged path to where I thought the Jeep was, my anxiety started to build. As we approached the gravel road close to the wreckage, Officer Taylor kept asking questions I still couldn't answer. It was almost like my life had started after the crash.

The road was a little confusing for me at first. It was hard to remember the way because there were only a few recognizable landmarks with a couple of intersecting paths. We eventually reached one narrow gravel road leading up from the foothills, and everything started looking more familiar. We got an incline that suddenly started winding more steeply, and I asked Officer Taylor to stop. I was relieved because I remembered this part of the path and the ascending slope next to the wreckage.

"Stop! It's somewhere around here."

Officer Taylor slowed to a stop and put his SUV Unit transmission in park and opened his door.

I got out and walked around the vehicle. I remembered my encounter with the snake and double-checked the surroundings. It brought back some unpleasant memories at first, and I stopped in my tracks.

"Are you okay?" Officer Taylor asked.

"Just give me a moment."

I then took a deep breath and walked back and forth, increasing the distance each time. Then I saw what looked like the ledge where the embankment was. I looked over the edge and couldn't see anything. I shook my head and started back to the Unit. Then I stopped abruptly. "The vehicle couldn't be seen when looking directly over the ledge," I thought.

I remembered going down about 10 yards to the east and then several steps down behind the ledge before seeing it the night of the accident. Even then, it wasn't easy to see it. I began tracing my steps toward the backside of the ledge.

Officer Taylor followed me. "Do you remember this place?"

I nodded as I walked towards the steep side of the ledge. I saw some rocks and then smiled as some taillights appeared. My shoes started losing their grip on the gravel, and I began sliding down the soft surface. I grabbed the side of the ledge and regained my balance before slowly edging down the slope.

"I see it!" I shouted.

Officer Taylor caught up to me, put his hand on my shoulder, and cautioned, "Be careful. Remember, you had a concussion. Take it easy."

After descending about 20 feet, I was overcome with emotions ranging from excitement to dread. I could now see the entire green and rusty upside-down Jeep.

I looked back and forth at Officer Taylor and then the Jeep.

"There it is," I said, pointing proudly at the wreckage.

Officer Taylor hurried towards the bottom of the embankment, and we both slipped and stumbled while finishing the descent. He grabbed my arm and ordered me to stay back so he could check the vehicle. At that moment I was surprised at what I saw. There was no license plate on the car after all. That didn't go unnoticed by Officer Taylor either. He turned and looked at me pleadingly.

"No license?"

I shrugged. "Why didn't it have one?" I thought. Was it a stolen vehicle? Did someone come back and take it off?"

Officer Taylor's approached the vehicle cautiously and removed a notepad from his shirt pocket and a pen. He pushed his hand towards me and said, "Move further back!"

Then he crouched and looked at the dashboard on the driver's side and scribbled some notes on the pad. When he stood up, he told me that the VIN number had been removed, making it difficult to find an owner. It probably had been stolen at some point.

Officer Taylor called dispatch for help to investigate the scene, and when another officer arrived, they canvased the entire area. After putting on latex gloves, they photographed the vehicle inside and out. After a complete search, they found no wallet or other identifying evidence, including identifying paperwork in the car. But there were some tennis shoe tracks that I hadn't noticed when I was there last. Officer Taylor had taken pictures of them as well. By now, I was discouraged and wanted to leave. My instincts were unsettled, and I was beginning to wonder if Officer Taylor might be having some doubts about me.

A single key was still in the ignition, so Officer Taylor retrieved it and placed it in a plastic evidence bag. In addition to the shoe prints, Officer Taylor photographed some fresh multiple boot prints around the car and on the embankment.

After returning to the gravel road, Officer Taylor went back and forth, checking for tracks. There appeared to be truck tire tracks that had passed over the area, covering the Jeep tracks, indicating that the vehicle came after the rollover.

I was overcome with fear and anxiety. Maybe I was one of the bad guys. Perhaps that's why my mind refused to remember. Maybe it was trying to protect me from the truth about me. If that was the case, I didn't want my memory to return.

Then Officer Taylor shook his head and said, "We have too many dots to connect. We need to find out why you had Ketamine in your system. I doubt you ingested it knowingly. You also had those marks on your wrists, suggesting that you were tied up and not there by choice. Someone or a group of people didn't want you alive. You could still be in danger if they know you are alive. Their biggest mistake is leaving you strapped in the seatbelt. It probably saved your life."

Before leaving, Officer Taylor reminded me that I should call him if I remembered anything. Then he said, "Let me know if you remember anyone from that might want to kill or harm you. There was plenty of Ketamine in your system, and you could have easily died."

He then urged me to keep a low profile until they learned more and to stay away from the crime scene.

What he said terrified me. All the while, I still worried that I could have been involved in a significant crime, and I felt like I was in danger. If that was true, I had no idea who would come after me or when it might happen. Worse yet, if someone wanted to kill me, they had probably already figured out that I was still alive. All they had to have done was read the Albuquerque Journal or watch the local news. I was a sitting duck.

Officer Taylor noticed my frightened expression and said, "Let's make sure that you're in a safe place with trustworthy people around you. I'll work on that."

That day, the Jeep was completely searched, towed from the mountains, and the little evidence there was collected.

The hospital arranged for a taxi to take me to the Albuquerque Shelter Center. It was on the westside of Albuquerque, funded by the city, with partnerships with the University of New Mexico for health care services. There was a barrack-style building connected to a sizeable cinder-block building. The main area had 50 beds, one right next to the other with narrow aisles between the rows. There was a respite area for persons like me who had recently been hospitalized and were still recovering. Despite being crowded, the facility was spotless. The facilities for the homeless seemed impressive. There was a computer lab, laundry facilities, showers, private areas for medical staff to do examinations, and a classroom and library. The beds were made of metal frames with compressed 4-inch-thick foam mattresses and vinyl-covered pillows. Folded, laundered sheets and blankets were on the bed assigned to me. At least I had a way to shower, had food, and a place to sleep. There were several male and female volunteers wearing name tags there. I found out later that they were mainly from a local church with the pastor, who was the director of the shelter.

At first, I was placed in the 30-bed respite area. I was also given a clean set of clothes sized by one of the volunteers to fit my build approximately. They included three changes of clothing gotten from a clothing bank, all donated by the community. Within an hour, the pastor from Morning Salvation Missionary Baptist Church visited the shelter and made his rounds. He eventually stopped for a special visit with me because he had been referred by Officer Taylor, who had been his friend since childhood and was a church member. Officer Taylor had briefed him about my circumstances.

Reverend Donald Myers was a portly man who appeared to be in his early to mid-sixties. His head was primarily bald, with short gray hair on the sides. He kept some thinning hair on the top combed neatly with gel across his scalp, giving him a neat and groomed appearance. A trimmed salt and pepper mustache neatly bordered at his upper lip and seemed bigger when he smiled. His brown eyes, thick clipped eyebrows, and steel-framed, rimless glasses gave him a professional appearance. Deep creases lined his tanned forehead, with a ridge above his eye sockets. His face was round, and he had a pronounced double chin. His faded blue jeans and navy-blue Polo shirt were extra-large to compensate for his enormous belly. His black leather orthopedic shoes were fastened at the top with Velcro straps, probably because it was too hard to navigate his midsection to tie his shoes.

Reverend Myers immediately interviewed me. His incredible deep radio voice struck me. It was pleasantly straightforward, and his diction made it easy to understand. He smiled and spoke with a lot of hand gestures while studying me. Everything about him made me relax, and for the first time since my nightmare began, I felt safe.

He seemed sincerely interested in me and my situation and kept eyeing me up and down as I answered his questions. He seemed to be trying to decide. My answers were the same for most of his questions. "I don't remember."

Finally, he put his hand up, gesturing for me to stop talking. He had heard enough. He then said he would revisit me once he finished his rounds.

After he left, I made my bed and watched a middle-aged homeless man with a volunteer pushing his wheelchair to a bed just two rows down. He had a Styrofoam food tray in his lap with a paper napkin and plastic fork on a tray. He was wearing a tattered baseball style hat covering his long thinning gray hair and a T-Shirt inside a long-sleeved blue flannel top. His donated blue jeans were a little too big, and his worn brown leather shoes had seen better days. I could see his big toe through a hole in the side of the shoe. He wasn't wearing any socks, and there were sores and scabs on his ankles. Secondhand shoes, clean socks, and a clean T-shirt were in a plastic bag on top of his bed.

At first, the man focused all of his attention on the food in his tray. But then he must have sensed that I was looking at him, and he turned towards me. I waved, and he waved back. His skin was tanned but had a yellowish tone, and his wrinkled face was beyond his age. He gave a half-smile revealing a missing front tooth as he reached under his tray and pulled out a folded Albuquerque Journal. He then waved it back and forth towards me.

"You wanna read this?" he asked.

I was surprised and asked, "Are you sure?"

The man gave a sarcastic expression and mockingly answered,

"Why do ya think I offered it, dumbass?"

He was right, and I was embarrassed, so I just shook my head, not knowing what to do next. It had suddenly become awkward.

"Go ahead and take it. I immediately reached and grabbed it. I done read it anyway," the man snapped and then tossed it onto the bed next to me.

"Thanks, man."

"It's nothin,"

The man then shrugged his shoulders and went back to chewing his food and sipping coffee from a Styrofoam cup. It made me wonder about him. I figured he probably had an interesting story to tell, but that would have to wait for another day. I didn't even ask his name.

Reverend Myers returned about an hour later after brief visits with several other homeless men and women. He shook my hand and sat down, motioning me to do the same. He said he had had a long discussion with Officer Taylor. He shared that they had a long trusting relationship that started when the young deputy was a teenager. He said they had agreed that I was a particular case that needed a haven until my memory returned.

At the end of our conversation, he surprised me by offering to take me to his home until I got better and maybe until I regained my memory. He emphasized that it was only temporary but had decided to take the chance on me because he was confident about judging a person's character. He had many years of working with people from many walks of life, and he had a good feeling about me. I wasn't his typical clientele and highly vulnerable because of my memory loss. He had decided that the chaotic environment at the shelter might interfere with my ability to regain memory and was less safe.

"After talking with Officer Taylor about your situation, I felt that the shelter might not be safe for you right now. To make it worse, you don't look very street smart to me, and you might not do well here. Besides, I have an extra bedroom at my house, and my neighbors look out for me. I've done this before, and they have been like family."

I was impressed with Reverend Myers' compassion. I was also surprised he was taking a chance on me without knowing much about my background. He seemed a perfect fit for running the shelter.

"I know this must be terrifying for you. We want you to get back on your feet and hope a more comfortable setting will speed up your recovery and memory. I hope this is okay with you."

I was relieved that my situation had just gotten so much safer because of two outstanding humanitarians and I agreed this move would probably help my memory come back sooner.

"Thank you. I don't know what to say."

"You'll get plenty of chances to say thanks," Myers chuckled. He then winked at me as we walked towards his vehicle.

"You'll earn your keep."

Reverend Myers opened the passenger door to his black 2015 Subaru SUV and quietly extended his hand towards the front passenger seat. I squeezed in and put my seatbelt on, and I took a deep breath. It reminded me of being suspended upside down just a few days earlier. My nose caught a faint smell of an Egg McMuffin, causing me to notice an empty McDonalds wrapper in a plastic bag hanging from around the bottom of the headrest. I suddenly felt hungry but didn't feel comfortable bringing it up. It could wait for now.

"Tell me more about Officer Taylor," I said.

Reverend Myers laughed as he put his seatbelt on. "He is the son of a close friend of mine who also goes to my church. Jim sometimes calls me Uncle Don. He's a good guy, and I've known him most of his life. We work well together. He's made a few referrals for special cases in the past, so you're not the first."

"Where are we going?"

"I live in the south valley, and it's a good neighborhood."

"So, how long will I be staying with you?"

"I decided to put you up at my house until you can remember enough to take care of yourself and find a place to live. It is quieter at my house, so you should mend quicker."

After about 15 minutes, Reverend Myers pulled into his driveway on Mesa, CT. SW. It was a typical one-story brown stucco three-bedroom flat-roofed house and xeriscaped with tan gravel in the front yard. There was a large Yucca plant in the center of the yard and matching Spanish brooms with yellow flowers on each front corner of the house. The pleasant scent from the flowers was like an inviting perfume as I approached the entrance. When I walked into the front room, I could see into the back yard through the sliding doors on the back wall of an efficiently furnished dining room. The backyard was primarily green grass surrounded by brown gravel and a rose garden with red, yellow, pink, and white roses lining the back-cinderblock wall. It was well-kept and pleasant to see. A small greasy-looking black barbeque grill was on the corner of the back porch and seemed out of place. It looked like he hadn't used it for some time, and somehow, it didn't fit the rest of the neatly landscaped yard. The butane tank had been disconnected from the fuel line and was hanging next to it.

The living room had a nice tan carpet and above the walnut-stained entry door was a crucifix. The ceiling was covered with tongue and grooved brown varnished ponderosa pine with equally spaced beams from end to end. The tan walls had a stucco texture, and there were pictures of a younger version of Reverend Myers with his arm around a nice-looking woman, who I presumed was his wife. He also had a black and white photo of an Albuquerque Dukes player, with Charlie Hough signed at the bottom and date 1969, next to his shoulder. There was a list of major league teams he must have played for at the bottom of the picture, including the Dodger, Rangers, White Sox, and Marlins.

Reverend Myers saw me studying the photo and said, "I met him through a friend, and he gave me that picture. He's now in the Hall of Fame. Had was a good pitcher and had a great knuckleball."

I nodded and asked, "Do you like baseball?"

"I go to a few games during the summer. The team now is called the Isotopes."

For some reason, that sounded familiar. I took a quick look around the room.

There were some framed prints of Vincent Van Gough paintings distributed throughout the living room. I pointed at the one with him and the young lady.

"So, is that your wife?" I asked.

"Yes. My wife died of cancer about a year ago, so it's just me," he answered.

"Oh, I'm sorry. I didn't mean..."

"Don't be. We were together for 33 years. We couldn't have children, but we were happy with the way things were. When she left this world, it was a blessing. She had suffered a lot, and it was hard for me. I can still feel her presence."

It was the first time I saw sadness in his eyes.

"Follow me and let me show you to your room."

"Sorry about your wife," I repeated.

"She was my soul mate, and there won't be another Mrs. Myers. She set the standard too high," he smiled. "It was hard for me at first, and I still have my moments, so I keep busy. That works the best."

"I wish I could have met her," I said.

"You would have liked her," he said. "I don't know how any person could have disliked her. She is my angel."

I smiled and said, "I can tell she was exceptional."

Myers took me into a small, spotless guestroom with a bed against the back wall and nightstands on each side. It had a landline phone on top of one of the stands. There was a mirror above the dresser on the wall opposite the bed on a clean but worn beige carpeted floor. The bed was covered with a white and blue handmade quilt with a foam pillow. A small closet with sliding doors and empty hangers inside was next to the dresser. A small 24" flat-screen TV was on the dresser, and a recliner with dark brown weaved fabric cushions stood in the corner next to one of the nightstands. The walls were painted with an off-white stucco textured surface. A simple green round ceramic-based table lamp with a tan triangular shade sat next to the phone on the nightstand. There were more recent photos on the wall of Reverend Myers and his wife.

The room had everything I needed for now, and I felt a deep sense of gratitude. The electric radio alarm showed 1:30 pm. I felt a headache coming on where the bump from the crash had been, and I felt exhausted, so I took my shoes off, laid on the soft mattress, and closed my eyes with my hands folded across my stomach and ankles crossed. I fell into a deep sleep almost immediately.

Reverend Myers peeked into the room around 5:00 pm and knocked on the door jam. I woke up with a start because I didn't recognize my surroundings initially. Then I remembered where I was and looked with a blank stare at Reverend Myers. He asked if I would like to eat. The mention of food reminded me that I was starving and thankful he had been so considerate. He had prepared a meal and set the table with paper plates and plastic flatware. His kindness was genuine, and I appreciated it. I felt fortunate to have met him and felt sure that he would always be my friend. When I smelled the seasoned hamburger meat and tomato sauce, it made me hungrier.

Reverend Myers smiled and said, "We have an exceptional meal with Hamburger Helpers. It's my specialty." Then he roared with laughter. I appreciated the humor and had to smile because it didn't matter. For me, it was a feast.

Once we were seated, he bowed his head and said a brief prayer of thanks for the food and asked for me to be blessed and for a quick return of my memory. As soon as he said, "Amen," his cell phone rang.

"I'd better get that."

He pulled out a smartphone from his shirt pocket and answered, "Hello…uh-huh, uh… he's right here. He handed the phone to me and

I looked at Reverend Myers inquiringly. He just nodded. I pulled it up to my ear and answered, "Hello?"

"Hi, It's Officer Taylor. I hope Reverend Meyers is taking good care of you. I just wanted to give you an update. We got your fingerprints back. The good news is that you're not a felon and have never been in jail. The bad news is there is no match. Our next hope is your DNA. We probably won't get it back for another two weeks. I'm sorry that we're not much closer to finding out who you are. You have a clear criminal background. Have you been able to remember anything yet?"

I paused for a couple of seconds and then answered, "I can't remember anything. I think the harder I try to remember things, the worse it gets."

"You're probably right. Relax. It'll start coming to you..."

"Listen, thanks for everything you've done for me," I interrupted. "I would be far worse off without your help and, of course, Reverend Myers. I don't know how to thank either of you."

"Don't worry about it. You'll get your chance. I'll keep in touch. Take care. Bye."

I gave the phone back to Reverend Myers and then ate the meal he had prepared. On this day, Hamburger Helpers was a gourmet dinner.

Reverend Myers handed me a Chromebook and told me to use it as often as I needed. He had gotten a few donated from his church to use for homeless persons. He said he had WIFI, so it was perfect for me to investigate anything that might come up about my past. He suggested looking up surnames to see if any might jog my memory.

I sat down and opened the Chromebook and realized I didn't remember very much about how to use it. I stared at it for a few minutes and Reverend Myers suddenly realized what was happening.

"I'm an old-timer and don't have a lot of skills, but I can show you the basics.

I nodded but kept staring at the screen as Reverend Myers sat next to me. Amazingly, I remembered some things about navigating the system. Once Reverend Myers prompted me on the parts that I had difficulty with, I started remembering enough to use the Google search engine.

I was very encouraged that I could navigate a Chromebook. Maybe things weren't so bad after all.

After about thirty minutes, Reverend Myers stood up and put his hand on my shoulder.

"I think you've got the hard parts down. If you need more help, just let me know, and I'll see if I can help. If I can't, I know a few people who could answer all your questions."

"Thank you... you've been so helpful; I don't know what to say."

"Thank you is good enough," Reverend Meyers said with a smile.

Before he left the room, he asked me if I would be willing to help at the Shelter on the following morning. I agreed immediately. It was the least I could do for all of the beautiful things he was doing for me. Besides, if I were working with Myers, I wouldn't be alone somewhere obsessing about my situation. After all, Reverend Myers had a lot of trust in me because he didn't know me. I laughed to myself, "Hell, I don't even know who Guy is!"

The following day Reverend Myers drove me to the Shelter to help with meals and giving out clothes. Several men and women were being served breakfast, and all of them looked like they had been homeless for a long time. They were happy to have a hot meal.

As Reverend Myers went to the front desk to check the census, I watched the men and women interacting with each other. Many were familiar with each other and seemed part of a small autonomous community. After a while, the tone shifted, and there was some name-calling between a few of the residents. Two volunteers stepped in and separated them.

"Some of these guys have to be watched closely. They can get aggressive if we don't keep order," Reverend Myers warned.

I nodded and watched more intently.

Reverend Myers started calling out names. Amazingly, he knew most of them by their first names. Sometimes he had to call them out multiple times, and sometimes he had to walk up to the person and put his hand on his shoulder to get their attention.

"Hey, Ken!"

When I heard the name, I turned around and started to respond to Reverend Meyers' voice. Right then, another older homeless man, answered, "Hi Reverend," as he walked toward the minister. I shook my head and laughed…, "Sorry, I thought you were talking to me."

Reverend Myers gave me a curious look and then turned back to his roster.

For a brief moment, I wondered if my name might be Ken. But I dismissed it because it didn't sound familiar anymore.

I helped with this service for a couple of weeks and built a positive dialogue with several homeless beneficiaries. Many had untreated mental illnesses or had refused to be treated. Many had drug addictions and were getting treatment through the shelter. While I appreciated the opportunity to give back to Reverend Myers' kindness, I was frustrated because nothing I did or learned gave me any clues about who I was. I had to remind myself to be more patient.

Overall, I was successful with most of the residents. When I got stuck, some of the volunteers would step in and help. It was evident that Reverend Myers had asked them to look out for me, and I was grateful for that too. For volunteers, it was not an easy job. Soon I began to realize how many of these individuals were victims of a system that sometimes tries to ignore them. I kept feeling like I needed to do more.

Officer Taylor called periodically but still had no new information. But hearing from him made me feel hopeful because I knew he was still working hard on the case.

I was also seeing Dr. George Duran, who had been assigned through the shelter program and who was helping me deal with some depression and anxiety. I had refused any medication, though. Dr. Duran had a very positive approach and insisted that my memory would eventually return. He recommended that I talk to him or someone I trusted if I felt overly anxious.

While my life was filled with anxiety and fear, I felt like some good people were helping me and that I was safer with them around me. I had been through a lot of trauma, and it would take some time to start feeling comfortable. It would help a lot if I could remember who I was and how I got into the situation that left me upside down in a Jeep in the mountains. Reverend Myers picked me up in his car and brought me back to his home. When we arrived, he told me that some the neighbors had noticed an increase of some suspicious vehicles passing through the neighborhood. A few had slowed down as if they were looking for someone.

"Don't worry. We have a real informal but effective neighborhood watch on this street. There are a lot of families with children, and nothing goes unnoticed."

That information worried me. I knew that I needed to pay more attention too.

Chapter 5

It had been almost four weeks since the accident on a Thursday morning, just a week before the July 4th holiday. My daily routine at the Shelter included working on the serving line at the Shelter during the day and then surfing the Internet at night to find something that might help me regain my memory. It left me exhausted and discouraged.

That night I had a nightmare. It was in bits and pieces, but it kept repeating itself. Two men were trying to beat me to death. I kept trying to escape but couldn't get away.

The following day, I woke up exhausted from the wrenching experience but got up anyway. I left for the Shelter as usual helped Reverend Myers with the food line. After I was finished serving, I ate some scrambled eggs, sausage, and toast and had some coffee with sugar and powdered creamer.

My wounds had mostly healed, and there wasn't any more physical evidence of the horrific incident. I left the Shelter to see Dr. Walsh at UNMH at 1:00 pm. I had taken the bus with some passes that Reverend Myers provided for homeless residents when they had medical appointments. He also gave me a temporary hand-made ID with the name "Guy X," but with a disclaimer based on my medical condition. By now, almost everyone I had met, including the homeless population, already referred to me as "Guy." The ID was practically worthless, except for providing evidence that I was somebody. It also served as an introduction to tell my story when I had an appointment.

Dr. Walsh was a practicing hypnotist. He appeared to be in his sixties and was heavy set with salt and pepper hair tied back into a ponytail and bald at the top. His appearance seemed to be a marketing strategy depicting him as someone more connected to celestial domains. It was not convincing for me. He wore a leisure black and white printed shirt with khaki shorts and brown leather sandals. His thick glasses were round with no rims. We had had had three sessions with little progress. Nothing but minor associations with city locations had surfaced thus far in my brain. Dr. Walsh was a patient man and was still pleased with my progress and urged me to be patient about my memory. He warned against trying too hard and assured me that my memory would probably return slowly and in bits and pieces. Finally, he urged me to relax so that I could maximize the sessions. While his advice seemed credible, it was mostly a repeat of everything he had told before.

After the appointment, I returned to the Shelter. Reverend Myers met me at the entrance and couldn't hide his alarm. He said that Officer Taylor had called with some surprising information. He said there was a breakthrough of some sort but felt it was better to get first-hand knowledge from Officer Taylor.

I hurriedly went to a phone in the dayroom area and called Officer Taylor. After three rings, Taylor answered.

"Hi, this is Guy. I understand that you have some important news."

"Yes, you'd better sit down first. This is gonna blow your mind. We have an exact match on your DNA test. It is for a Kelly Garrity. His prints were on file and were similar to yours but not an exact match, so we think he may be your identical twin. The problem is, he died a few days ago in El Paso from an overdose of heroin. He had several previous arrests for drug-related charges and burglaries. Interestingly, the drug charges were for selling significant quantities of heroin, not using it. He had no history as a user. El Paso PD is convinced he was a dealer. He has no extended family members listed on any of his available records. We received a fax with his picture. He looks just like you. He has to be your identical twin. I'll show it to you when I see you. By the way, law enforcement in El Paso says there's evidence that Kelly's overdose was forced on him. There is physical trauma. El Paso PD believes he was murdered because of a drug deal gone wrong. They had beaten him severely. He was a known small-time dealer.

I was overwhelmed. "A twin? I have or had a twin brother, but he's dead."

I couldn't speak because my head was spinning. I wondered if I was caught up in a drug trafficking ring with my brother and if we had both been marked for murder or maybe killed him by mistake for something I had done. Now I wouldn't get any information about our pasts from him either or see him alive. It was just too much information to process.

After catching my breath, I asked, "So what's next?"

"We're going to look at all of his records, including juvenile, to see what else we can find out. We might find something on him if we can access each state's vital records, starting with Texas and New Mexico. We might be able to find you too. I think we can safely assume that your last name is probably Garrity unless Kelly had changed his name at some point. But he has no record of aliases. I'll update you as I learn more. I'll also show you the results and pictures of him as soon as we can get together. By the way, we were able to recover DNA for two other persons inside the Jeep on the turn signal and the driver's side door. We ran them through the lab but came up empty. That doesn't mean it won't be valuable in the future. As this case goes on, we may find some persons of interest that match them. That could bust it wide open.

By now, I'm sure that Officer Taylor had noticed my silence. "Are you okay?"

"A... yeah.... thank you. I'm just overloaded right now. I think I'll be doing some research of my own with Detective Google."

Taylor smiled. "You can call me Jim from now on. I think we'll be exchanging a lot of information in the future. Are you sure you're gonna be alright?"

"I will eventually. I have to get my head around it."

At that moment, my mind was racing. I wondered, "What were Kelly and my relationship as brothers?" It was going to haunt me until I remembered who we were.

"Okay, Jim, I'll be waiting to hear from you again soon,"

By now, my brain was on overload. It was unbelievable.

Officer Taylor now had a better read on me from watching my behavior. He had noticed different characteristics and was building a profile. He had guessed that I probably had more than a high school education in some of our conversations, based on my vocabulary. He was also convinced that I hadn't been dishonest with him or Reverend Myers. He had mentioned this to me more than once. He thought these observations might come in handy at some point.

I couldn't stop thinking about it that day and had difficulty sleeping that night. I couldn't understand how so many parts of my brain could be intact while there was so much missing. But despite the terrible news about my brother, getting closer to my identity gave me more reason for hope.

The following day, Jim called. "I have the best news for you yet. We were able to get birth certificates on Kelly and you, Kenneth!"

I looked up for a second, recalling the time I almost answered that name.

"Unbelievable! So, my name is Kenneth Garrity for sure?"

"Without a doubt," Jim answered. "You should be very excited. Does that name jog any memories?"

I took a deep breath and thought about it for a few seconds. "Nope, not a damn thing comes to me, but the other day Reverend Myers called that name for one of the homeless men, and I answered him. But I just blew it off. At the time, I thought I had misheard because there was a lot of noise and arguing between some of the residents. Now I'm sure there was more to it."

"That's encouraging," Jim replied. "Hopefully, this is bringing your memory back."

"I agree. It gives me something to work with. I guess you should start calling me Ken from now on," I laughed.

"Sure thing, Ken. I'll talk to you again soon," Jim said as he hung up.

I felt excited and encouraged. It caused me to immediately think about finding out more about myself, starting with the DMV. "It'll only be a matter of time," I thought.

While at the shelter, my outlook was much more optimistic the rest of the day. I was unusually cheerful in my dealings with the clientele and visitors. But once I returned to Reverend Myers' residence, my headache had returned. I was sure it was because my mind was in overdrive, and my mental confusion was getting in the way. It was just too much information, and yet, not enough. I took some Tylenol and laid back on the bed. I didn't feel like eating, so after giving the details about what I had learned to Reverend Myers, I told him I was turning in. I was still worried that Ken Garrity might be a bad guy. It was a good thing I was exhausted from it all because I slept without waking the entire night. There were no dreams remembered the following day, but I was still felt tired and needed some coffee to wake me up.

I smelled the faint scent of freshly cut grass from outside and could hear a gas lawnmower. I could see daylight flooding the room through the window blinds, and the warmth comforted me.

My mind started racing again as I considered different approaches to discover more about myself. I leaned over to the bottom of the window next to his bed and separated the white vertical blinds carefully with my fingers. I saw Reverend Myers with a wide-brimmed straw hat, sunglasses, and garden gloves pushing the mower in the front yard. He was wearing jeans, a white T-Shirt, and old brown leather work boots. Soon after arriving at his residence, he told me that yard work was part of his Saturday morning ritual. Saturdays were always busy. He included a brief visit to the shelter in the afternoon followed by trips to the homes of any parishioners who needed his attention.

I glanced up and down the block and saw two young boys riding up and down the street on their Mongoose bicycles. A few houses down, I saw a young Hispanic man with short-cropped black and gray hair and sunglasses sitting behind the steering wheel of a late black model Lincoln Continental, scrolling his smartphone with his index finger, probably waiting to give a ride to someone. A mail carrier was also working his way down the street in his postal truck.

I sat up and waited to see if my headache would return. After about a few minutes, I was relieved that it appeared to be gone. I was also hungry, so I got up, showered, put on some donated Wrangler jeans with a pullover blue T-Shirt, and went into the kitchen. I then read a posted note that said, "There is a frozen breakfast burrito in the freezer wanting you to eat it, or you can have some cereal from the cupboard." I opened the freezer door of the refrigerator and pulled out the frozen breakfast burrito. I placed it in the Microwave and programmed it for 2 minutes. After the loud beeps alerted me that it was finished cooking, I put it on a paper towel and poured some hot coffee into a mug that had been left on the counter next to the sink. After adding a packet of artificial sweetener and milk from the refrigerator, I sat at the dining room table. Reverend Myers had left the Albuquerque Journal on the counter, so I thumbed through the pages, reading the headlines, as I sipped the hot coffee. The coffee tasted extra well, and I could feel energy returning to my body from the caffeine. Reverend Myers had finished the jumble word puzzle from section B and had spilled some coffee on the page. It brought a smile to my face as I envisioned him just shrugging his shoulders and haphazardly dabbing it with a paper towel.

I read the paper from cover to cover while I ate the burrito. It would have tasted better if I had waited until it cooled down instead of constantly blowing on it and still burning my tongue. I eventually had to cut it into pieces with a fork. The taste seemed very familiar, and the spices added to the heat. Even though it had damaged my tongue's taste buds, it satisfied my hunger and left a good aftertaste in my mouth. I poured the last cup of coffee from the pot and sat at the table for several minutes, thinking about what to do next.

After I washed and dried the dishes in the sink, I stood up and stretched, noticing how meticulous the Reverend was at organizing the cabinets. He kept everything in the kitchen spotless, so I was careful to clean off the table and counter before throwing the garbage into the rubber trash bin inside the cabinet next to the sink.

I then put on the black baseball cap given to me at the shelter. The words "Walmart" were displayed on the front with blue lettering. As I closed the door and entered the front yard. I walked towards Reverend Myers, and he stopped the mower when I came into view.

"Can I help you with any of this," I asked?

He smiled and answered, "I think you should take the day off, Ken. Do something different that's relaxing. Do something new. Next week, I'm going to start paying you for working at the shelter. You have been working very hard, and I know you need some income. But there are no benefits, like retirement, or anything like that, just the knowledge you're doing something for those in need."

"No," I replied. "You have done more than enough for me. I can't ask you to pay me when you're giving me a place to stay food to eat," I pled.

Myers defiantly tilted his head, "You didn't ask me," he countered.

"This isn't a negotiation. Let me have my way. I'm a minister, and I won't take no for an answer," he quipped. He then smiled broadly snapped, "No more discussion on this!"

I shrugged my shoulders and replied, "Well ... okay then, but I don't know what I'll do today."

Doing something different was easier said than done. I wasn't motivated to go anywhere, so I watched some local television shows, including the news. I couldn't think of anything other than to start researching my case.

I started to explore the Internet to see if there were any records of me but was interrupted by Reverend Myers. He came to my room and handed me some free tickets for an Albuquerque Isotopes baseball game. His demeanor was more commanding than just making an offer.

"The Isotopes organization donated these. You do like baseball, right?"

He handed me $20.00 to get hotdogs and soft drinks and put his right hand on my shoulder. "This is just what the Dr. is ordering for you," he grinned.

The Isotopes were playing against El Paso. The stadium was located near downtown Albuquerque off of University Blvd., next to Central New Mexico Community College and just south of the University of New Mexico, located on Central Avenue. I shrugged my shoulders and agreed to go. I went to the bathroom, took a shower, put on my clothes, and combed my hair. Reverend Myers drove me to the bus stop even though it was just a few blocks away. He then handed me a cheap cell phone that he had purchased with one hour of minutes on it that he had paid in advance. He said it was for emergencies and on the back was a post-it note with the phone number scribbled on it. I thanked him and was overwhelmed by his kindness.

I got on the bus when it arrived and stopped just south of Coal Ave. I then walked to the stadium a few blocks away.

The Isotopes were hot that night and beat El Paso 10-2. It was fun to watch since there were many hits, and I had to concede that Reverend Myers had a lot of wisdom pushing me into this activity. It turned out that recreation was just what I needed. It took my mind off all the chaos in my life. The ride back home was relaxing too.

When I got off the bus and started walking back to Reverend Myers' address, I was calmer and noticed a lot more about my surroundings. There were a lot of young children going up and down the sidewalks on scooters and bicycles. Two older teens were playing catch in the middle of the street. There were two teens on skateboards, too, and they waived at me. The noises were all happy sounds.

As I got closer to my temporary home, I noticed that the man in the Lincoln sedan was again waiting in front of the same house. I looked at him for several seconds to make eye contact, but the man was too fixated on his smartphone. He acted as if he was unaware that I existed.

When I arrived at Reverend Meyers' address, I noticed that the front door was open but locked the screen door. I rang the doorbell and looked back at the Lincoln again. It was gone. It made me feel a little suspicious, and I took a mental note to watch for him.

Reverend Myers appeared at the door with a glass of iced tea in his hand. Myers smiled and asked, "...Well?"

I laughed, "You were right. It was just what the Dr. ordered. I feel much better now."

"Come on in and have some tea and we'll talk about your j-o-b," said Myers sarcastically.

We discussed the following week's activities and what I would be doing. Reverend Myers was paying me minimum wage. I couldn't transport because I didn't have a driver's license yet. But there was plenty of work to do at the shelter, like serving meals and helping with clean-up. Some of it would be handling the bickering between residents that often occurred.

I asked him if he had seen the black Lincoln Continental and driver before.

Reverend Myers laughed, "That's my neighbor's ex-husband picking up his son for the day. You'll see him every Saturday while you're here," He explained.

I was relieved and felt like I might be a little paranoid, but it was warranted considering my circumstances. My reality had made me hypersensitive. I had so much to think about, and there were a lot of random puzzle pieces. I knew it would be on my mind at all times until my memory was fully restored. Even though they told me that it might take longer to get my memory back, I couldn't stop thinking about it despite all the advice to stop obsessing about it. The frustrating part was that when I caught a glimpse of something familiar in my memory, it would disappear in a flash. Then I couldn't recall much of it.

Even though the Lincoln sedan wasn't anything to worry about, it reminded me that it was probably a good idea to pay close attention to my surroundings at all times. It was extra scary because I still didn't know what or for whom I was looking. I decided that from now on, I was going to focus on people that I came into contact with and for anything that looked out of place.

I went for a walk through the immediate neighborhood and made a mental note of all the people I saw. The fresh air gave me a sense of well-being and allowed me to think more clearly. It appeared that the neighborhood had a friendly community atmosphere. I waved at a few of the neighbors, and they waved back. When I returned to the house, I was tired and sat in the chair, turned on the TV in the living room and immediately fell asleep.

Chapter 6

Jane Connors was 22 years old and had finally landed a good enough job to leave her parent's home and live independently. Her parents had been very helpful to her and never complained about her living with them once she turned twenty-one. Almost six months ago, injuries from an automobile accident had caused her to spend a lot of time in bed, and her recovery was slow. The doctor had recently told her that she had recovered totally and there were minimal scars. She was a very attractive woman with long, wavy, orange-red hair and had a curvy physique with an engaging personality, making her even more appealing. Her fair skin was covered with freckles, and her Texas accent was soft and charming. Her blue framed glasses matched her ocean blue eyes.

Jane had lived in Albuquerque for most of her life, but her parents were from Austin, Texas. She was an only child, so her parents were willing to do anything to help her. Her father was a big man with white hair and a big waistline. He had an unmistakable Texas drawl. His name was Jack. He had his own construction business and made a good living. Her mother, like Jane, had red hair, but it was short and straight. She had a petite frame, blue eyes, and fair skin, but she had very few freckles. Her name was Rosemary. She was quiet and worked on and off in real estate to stay busy and help with the family income. She was a smart and caring woman who was a good match for her husband's big personality.

Jane was excited about her new job as a Health Services Human Resource Assistant at Presbyterian Hospital in Rio Rancho, New Mexico. She was also excited about her quest to find an apartment. It was a new start and adventure, leaving her completely independent. She had finally recovered from a horrible automobile accident and was feeling normal again. The injuries to her head and her left leg hadn't done permanent damage, but it had complicated her life and had put a halt to some of her plans. She was also recovering from a heartbreaking end to a serious relationship.

About a year earlier, Jane was employed as a secretary and was in a serious relationship with a promising good-looking young college student. They had even talked about marriage. He was a year younger, but his self-discipline, good looks, and personality made him seem older. Her parents liked him too.

Ken, her boyfriend, was an artist and musician and was a straight "A" college student. One night Jane and some of her friends had attended one of his singing performances, and he approached her afterward. He was friendly and seemed to be a good person. He told her he hadn't made a lot of money from music but liked writing music, singing, and playing the guitar. He was working towards a degree in Fine Arts from a local community college and was almost finished. His main goal was to work as a commercial artist. While working on his degree, he was employed at his college under a Work-Study program in the maintenance department. He had lost his father two years earlier, and then his oldest brother and mother had died within the past year, and was still grieving. He didn't have any close family members left and avoided talking about the losses. Jane had tried to be supportive, knowing that he would have to deal with it eventually.

Soon after Jane and Ken started seeing each other, he asked her to start going with him for his performances on a Saturday at a Coffee Shop in Corrales, just north of Albuquerque. It was called "Welcome Home." Saturdays drew bigger audiences. Several up-and-coming musicians performed there. Ken only earned from donations by those who had come to have tea a meal enjoy some local music. The donations weren't much more than when a performer on the street puts his hat on the ground to collect money. But it didn't seem to matter to Ken because he liked the experience. Ken had shared that he had severe stage fright, so it was a friendly place to help him overcome it. His guitar skills were pretty good, but it was his voice that people came to hear. He was able to switch back and forth from rock to classical and had a pleasant tone.

While she was at a performance, Jane met Ken's close friend, Sam Zachery, and his girlfriend, Katie Harmon. After a few more performances, she got to know them well. Ken and Jane started going to Sam's two-bedroom trailer to have a few drinks and visit after performances. Ken and Sam had been friends for some time. Sam had even written the lyrics to one of the songs Ken sang that night.

Sam was the same age as Ken and worked on getting a trade in plumbing from the same school as Ken. He had written a lot of good poetry and had an impressive collection. He had offered to help Ken with lyrics for some of his songs, and they had found it easy to work together.

Sam was good-looking and had a big ego to match. He flirted with every girl he encountered, including Jane, and it bothered her because he did it right in front of Katie.

Ken and Sam did a lot of partying at Sam's and Katie's trailer. It was a lot of fun, and they drank and listened to a lot of music.

Sam and Katie were not the typical couple. Sam looked like a male model, while Katie was very plain. She didn't wear much makeup, and she was not physically fit like he was. She was about 5'2' with sandy blonde hair and hazel eyes. She preferred casual attire and usually wore baggie jeans and plaid shirts with tennis shoes or sandals. She got most of her attractiveness from her sweet personality. She worked as a cashier at Walmart and shared the trailer with Sam for about a year. For now, Katie was the primary income for them, and she was the signed tenant of the trailer. Sam didn't contribute much but promised to become the primary wage earner once he got certified as a plumber. When he did earn money, it was either from crafts he had made or selling weed. The landlord was not aware he was living there full time but never checked, so it was an excellent arrangement for the two of them.

Katie and Sam's relationship seemed to work. Katie had a very engaging personality, and that, coupled with the financial stability, seemed to be the main attraction for Sam. It gave him the strength he needed to take his time getting a trade while living a carefree lifestyle. She helped to keep him grounded and often talked him out of impulsive money ventures.

Jane and Katie eventually became good friends. They often met for coffee and sometimes went for drinks. Katie was mainly happy with Sam despite his openly flirtatious behavior. But sometimes, she would complain about it privately with Jane when they were alone.

Over a few months, Jane had connected with Ken. They spent a lot of time together and enjoyed each other's companionship. Jane knew they both cared for each other. While Ken had his own house outside of Albuquerque, he lived alone. He had gotten ill at one point during their time together, and she and her parents had let him stay at their house until he recovered. She helped him get better. He had suffered from chronic spasms in his colon, and it was very painful, but they eventually went away. She was confident that the illness was connected with Ken's facing the deaths in his family. She never brought it up or tried to discuss it with him because he seemed unwilling to talk about it.

Ken continued to perform and spend a lot of time with Sam and Katie but had started shifting more and more attention to his education. It had become his highest priority. Sam was the most outgoing of the two, and he liked mischief. That caused a dilemma for the more conservative nature of Ken, and Sam had some influence over him. That was Ken's eventual downfall. He had followed Sam's lead one too many times. Eight months after he started dating Jane, Ken betrayed her. She found out about it because Sam told Katie, and she had to confront Ken before he came clean.

One night after a performance at a local Coffee House, Ken and Sam had gone to a restaurant and had some coffee, as they often did. While they were there, two older nice looking Hispanic women in their early '40s came into the restaurant and sat in the booth across from them. Both women were wearing short skirts that exposed their sexy legs. While they ordered some desert, one of them had her eyes fixated on Sam. The women looked a little drunk, and it appeared they had been bar hopping and still looking for some action. One of them had a low-cut blouse that exposed most of her well-proportioned breasts and was the prettier of the two. Sam couldn't contain himself, and his eyes were laser-focused on her. He started flirting with her, seductively licking a strawberry from his slice of pie before putting it in his mouth and rolling it around with his tongue. He sipped his coffee while gazing over the cup at her with a smile. She was interested and was flirting back.

Supposedly, Sam had suggested that he and Ken go and sit with them. Ken later claimed that it had made him uncomfortable, but he had gone along with Sam's constant urging anyway. He couldn't explain why but Jane saw it as weak. As the flirting continued, they all sat together joking and laughing. Ken said he had noticed that Sam already had his hand wedged comfortably between the legs of the one he was sitting next to. Finally, she suggested that they leave the restaurant and follow them to their apartment. They all agreed.

After arriving at the appointment Sam started passionately kissing the woman he was with and slowly backed her into the bedroom as he fondled her. Ken eventually told Jane that her name was Olivia. He and the other woman, whose name was Rachael, could hear the heavy breathing and squeals from Olivia as they sat together engaging in small talk. After a while, Ken said that Sam and Olivia returned to the living room, and they all partied for a while longer, drinking more wine. Sam started flirting with Rachael and eventually sat next to her. He started kissing her, and it was apparent she was his next conquest. Ken said that Olivia then sat next to him and started touching him. He admitted that he gave in at that point. Jane didn't believe that he was that innocent about it.

After about an hour of drinking, Sam took Rachael's hand and headed to the bedroom. Supposedly, Sam motioned Ken and Olivia to join them. According to Ken, when they went into the bedroom

Sam and Rachael were on the floor, and he was already on top of her, thrusting passionately, causing her to whine and moan.

Jane pressured Ken for details. He said that Olivia coaxed him to the bed. Once there, she started kissing and caressing him. She took her clothes off and started removing his. From there, things got heated. But then, according to Ken, his conscience took over, and he apologized to Olivia, stopping her advances. He said he couldn't because he felt it wasn't right to cheat on his girlfriend. Olivia didn't seem to get offended and had acted as if she understood. They returned to the living room without having sex, but Ken had done enough to damage his relationship with Jane.

Sam caused Ken to wait for another hour because he and Racheal continued having sex in the bedroom. He was surprised and impressed by Sam's endurance. Immediately after they returned to the living room, Ken took Sam home and went back to his own house.

After hearing Ken's side of it, Jane was livid and didn't believe most of what he had said. She couldn't think that somehow things were okay because he ultimately avoided the final sex act.

Jane decided to break up with Ken. He had crossed the line in their relationship, and she felt he had another side, making it impossible to trust him.

According to Katie, Ken had confronted Sam, and there was a heated argument. It turned out that Sam had only told her about the fling because he had found out that he had gotten gonorrhea from one of the two women. Both Sam and Katie had to be treated for it. Sam had urged Ken to get tested. Ken took the test to prove to Jane that he hadn't had sex. He had told Jane about the results hoping it would mitigate his shameful act. But she wasn't impressed.

Sam had the upper hand in his and Katie's relationship and never seemed to worry about the situation. Even though she was angry and disgusted, Katie forgave him. But she was deeply hurt.

Jane distanced herself from them because Sam knew better, and Katie seemed weak. She had recently started talking to Katie again, only because she had finally broken up with Sam after he had cheated on her again.

Jane had felt Ken's betrayal was unforgivable and that she could never trust him again. Sam claimed that the idea of going to Olivia and Rachael's apartment was all Ken's idea but didn't believe that either.

Ken had apologized repeatedly and begged for a second chance. He had gotten the STD test and proved he hadn't had sex with either of the women. He said that he had also contacted the two women to warn them about the STDs. When he called them back, they both admitted they tested positive and were being treated. But Jane was angry and said she didn't care anymore. The test didn't mean anything because Ken was with another woman, and that was his responsibility.

To be safe, Jane got tested and was negative for STDs. But she was wounded, and Ken was heartbroken. He seemed resigned because he was guilty and had no defense, so he walked away. He had told Jane that he was disappointed in himself for being weak and easily influenced and was sad that things had turned out the way they did.

Jane went back to work and tried to leave Ken in her past. As for Ken, he had gone back to school, and she had hoped he had learned a life lesson. She knew he had friends in the works study program, and his supervisors were middle-aged blue-collar men. They would console him and hopefully counsel him about learning from his mistakes.

Almost a week later, Jane started having second thoughts. After thinking it over, she remembered that their relationship had been very good before Ken had betrayed her. More importantly, she still had strong feelings for him. She started believing that Ken was sincere when he told her it would never happen again. Trust had been seriously damaged, though, and if they got back together, it would take some work to repair the damage. After mulling over what happened and the pain she had endured from the separation, she called him while he was at work and told him she wanted to talk. She asked if he could come to her work at "Lights and Lamps" in Rio Rancho to talk. Ken sounded very excited, and he agreed immediately.

A little after 5:00 pm Ken parked his car in front of her job site. Everyone had left work for the day except Jane. He appeared very happy to meet with her. When he came into the store, Jane was surprised that he was clean-shaven and had gotten a short haircut, which was not his normal look. He had had a beard and long hair the whole time they had been together. Jane had tried to get him to try a more conservative look, but he had resisted because he felt it was suitable for his musical appearances. She thought he looked very handsome, with his new haircut.

They had talked for almost an hour and eventually agreed to give their relationship another try. Jane had given him a stern warning that this would be his only chance and that another betrayal would cost him the relationship for good. He apologized several times and seemed eager to give it another try. She invited him to come to her house at 7:00 pm that night so they could go out for coffee and talk some more. He agreed and seemed very relieved.

Jane was happy. She had shown him her new car. It was a small Honda N360. It looked like a cute breadbox on wheels. Her parents had put a down payment on it for her. Ken had reminded her to be careful because it was small and probably wouldn't hold up too well in an accident. She reminded him that her old car, a little MG, was even smaller.

Jane had no idea that Ken's warning would foretell the unfortunate events later that day. For the moment, she was excited, and Ken seemed happy for her. After they finished looking at the car, they kissed and hugged, and she said she would be leaving within the next ten minutes to go home. He waved at her and left immediately. Jane locked the door of her reception area, got into her new car, and pulled out onto Highway 528, heading south. After driving a quarter of a mile, a car suddenly turned left right in front of her. She didn't have time to stop before she felt intense pain, and everything went black.

Ken later told her that when he had gone to her house at 7:00 pm, no one was there. This had been unusual because her mother and father were always home by 5:30 in the evening on workdays. He had gotten worried, and after waiting for an hour, he sensed something was wrong started calling the local hospitals. His instincts had proven correct because he found out she was at Presbyterian hospital on Central Ave. The emergency room wouldn't tell him why she was there. He rushed to the hospital and found out what room she was in. When he got there, her parents were at her bedside. They acted surprised to see him. It was obvious her parents were unaware that Ken and Jane had gotten back together. Jane was conscious. When she saw him, she smiled and said, "Hi Ken, when did you get your hair cut? It looks nice." She was pleased to see him, but she had had a head injury and wasn't clear-headed. Jane's parents had told Ken that Jane had partial amnesia. She couldn't remember the accident or anything that had happened in the recent past but was happy that Ken was there. She had hit her head during the auto accident and was seriously injured both to the head and left leg. Her left leg was broken in two places. Her parents had told Ken that the head injury was severe but that the Dr. said that she would recover. They also noted that her partial memory loss would probably return soon. Jane hadn't remembered their breakup or its causes.

For Jane, it was expected, but for Ken, it was awkward and caused anxiety. She had gone home two days later and spent most of her time on a couch in her parent's living room with her casted leg propped up on a chair. The first few days, she was sick and in pain. He had come to her house every day for a week after she got home. He had been very supportive.

After the first week, Ken started pressuring her about her memory. It was subtle at first but more evident as the days passed. She felt he didn't believe she had forgotten about their breakup and eventual reconciliation. His impatience had irritated her. It caused her to have second thoughts about continuing their relationship. She had tried to tell Ken to be patient, but his continued pressure was mounting.

Because of his behavior, she started dreading his visits. She grew impatient with him and decided that he was more worried about himself than her, and she got angry. Two weeks after the accident, she finally yelled at him and called him a "selfish son of a bitch!" Then she told him to leave and never come back. She couldn't take it anymore.

This time he looked very defeated and left without a word. He hadn't tried to contact Jane since that day. But she also had a dark secret. As it turned out, Ken was right. Even though she had lost her memory from the accident, she had regained it in just a few days. But because she was injured and would have scars on her leg, she wondered how faithful Ken would be if she was permanently disfigured. When he pressured her, it pushed her away more, but now she realized that she should have been honest about her memory. If Ken had known about her lie, it would have created more conflict, and in her condition, she hadn't been mentally capable of resolving it.

All of that drama was now Jane's biggest regret. When she started feeling better, she realized that she had over-reacted and missed Ken. More importantly, she was in love with him. She tried several times to contact him, but he didn't answer. She even called his best friend, Sam. Surprisingly, Sam had laughed at her and told her that he and Ken were no longer friends, and he had no idea where Ken was. He was rude and said Ken was just a leach and she was stupid for wanting him back. He told her that she needed to stop calling him and that he never liked her. That was a total shock to her. It was a side of Sam that she hadn't seen before, especially since he seemed so close to Ken.

Sam was no longer with Katie by then too. He had met someone else, and Katie caught him cheating with her. According to Katie, his new girlfriend, Becky, had met Ken and didn't like him either. She gave Sam an ultimatum to stop hanging around with Ken, or she was going to leave. She seemed to have a lot of power over him. Katie said that Sam turned against Ken and told him he didn't want to be around him anymore. He had been insulting. Katie noted that Ken stood his ground with Sam for the first time and had told him off." Katie said she was surprised because Ken was not confronting Sam at all.

Jane always thought Sam was jealous of Ken because he was so disciplined, talented, and dedicated to getting his education. Sam was a big talker but didn't follow through on his goals. He always relied on his good looks to get what he wanted. Ironically, Ken was just as good-looking, but he didn't seem to know it. She also didn't trust Sam. Katie sometimes worried about some of his drug dealings. She saw a few of them, and they looked dangerous.

Katie had provided Sam with financial support the whole time they had been together, and it appeared the same thing was happening with his new girlfriend.

It was good that Ken and Sam weren't friends anymore, but she had lost all contact with Ken as a result. She thought about looking for him at the college but decided against it. He would probably be unwilling to try working things out now, and it was too public.

Jane was very discouraged but figured that there might be an opportunity to patch things up sometime later after things cooled off, but their chances would die if she waited too long. She decided she would try to reach Ken again if she found out where he was. When they had broken up, he had bought a home, and she didn't know where it was and couldn't locate his name on the internet. He was probably furious and hurt. In the meantime, she decided to concentrate on her new job to get an apartment and start living independently.

Jane was a hard worker, and she impressed her boss with how quickly she learned her new job during that first week. She started saving money so she would have enough to maintain her apartment. Jane's father told her that he and her mother would cover the initial deposit and first month's rent once she had found an apartment she liked and could afford.

She could have her own "home" sooner than later. She had found a two-bedroom apartment that she could decorate to make it feel like her.

Rita, a friend she had kept in touch with from high school, urged her to go out and celebrate her new job, but Jane told her that she wanted to wait until she ultimately moved into her new apartment and finished setting it up. She had picked out the apartment in Rio Rancho, New Mexico, about 10 miles northwest of Albuquerque.

During the weekend, Sam's old girlfriend, Katie, contacted Jane to catch up. They hadn't spoken for a while, but they continued their friendship after their breakups. Katie told her that she had lost contact with Sam. Katie told Jane how she and Sam broke up. She hadn't broken up just because of his infidelity, even though she had to be treated for gonorrhea. But Katie cared about him and forgave him. She realized now that she should have known better. Sam still had all his personal belongings in her trailer and had assured her that he was ready to make a total commitment to their relationship. They had been living mostly on what she earned at Walmart, but Sam was looking for a full-time job for a plumbing company.

Katie said that out of nowhere, Sam met another woman online. Her name was Becky Espinosa. Becky had a well-paying job with a good position at a bank and was drop-dead gorgeous. So, Sam cheated again but told her the relationship was over. Katie immediately kicked him out of the trailer and threw his belongings outside. He had made a scene outside when he came to get the belongings, but he just picked them up and loaded them in his car and left when she didn't answer the door. Becky had already invited Sam to move out of the trailer and into her house anyway, so he did.

Katie then broke her lease and moved back in with her parents temporarily but saved some money and moved to a small apartment within the following week. She said she was agitated and had felt used. But Katie also said Sam had been getting involved with selling more illegal and dangerous drugs, so she was relieved that he wasn't exposing her to his new friends. She lamented that he had frequently "sold weed," but now he was selling coke and Ecstasy, and maybe some other things. He had become more and more secretive before breaking up, but she was suspicious because of the extra money he was bringing in.

When she learned that Jane was looking for an apartment, Katie offered to let her share hers. It was small but had two bedrooms.

Jane declined and said that she had wanted something with more space and needed to be on her own. She also needed time to work things out for herself and was excited about becoming fully independent.

Jane signed the lease on her new apartment a week later. Her parents kept their word and gave her the money she needed to move in. They took care of the deposit. It took her a week more to get her things moved in. As a bonus, her parents bought her some expensive matching southwestern furniture for the living room. Now she had enough to buy her bedroom furniture, and she bought the dining room table and chairs on credit.

Jane enjoyed arranging and decorating it to her taste. She had added reds, oranges, and yellows wherever she could but felt some sadness and took a deep breath when she hung up an oil painting of her miniature poodle that Ken had given her for her birthday, and it made her feel sad.

That Friday night, Rita came and helped her celebrate with some red wine and cheese. They drank until their words were slurred and almost incomprehensible. Rita agreed to stay overnight. She was hammered, and it was the safest thing to do.

The following day Jane and Rita got up after 10:00 am. The hangovers had slowed them down. Jane drank a big glass of water to counter the thirst and dehydration. Rita spent some time over the toilet throwing up what she had eaten and drank the night before. They eventually had some coffee and turned on her new 45" Samsung wide-screen TV and stayed there for two hours without comprehending the TV shows in front of them while recovering from dehydration and headaches.

Jane picked up her laptop computer and started scrolling through the headlines. Suddenly, her eyes widened like silver dollars. As she read and saw the pictures, she started sobbing. As she got louder, Rita hurried into the room and asked, "What's wrong?"

Jane pointed at the computer screen and cried, "Look!"

Rita stared at the screen and read the story under the headlines. She asked, "Ken? Look, they got his first name wrong. They identified him as Kelly!"

Jane continued to cry. After regaining her composure, she told Rita that she had been trying to reach him to see if they could get back together. Now she knew why she hadn't been able to reach him. He must have moved to El Paso. She was in disbelief that he died from a heroin overdose. Jane looked at Rita and said, "Ken used to smoke weed with Sam, but I never knew him to do any other drugs. It doesn't sound right. Maybe there was more that I didn't know about him, but I think I would have noticed heroin addiction."

Rita continued to read the story, "You're right. You may not have known him as well as you thought. It says here that he had a criminal background, including selling drugs."

"What?"

Jane was in shock. She couldn't accept that he was dead.

Rita asked, "Do you think Sam knows about this?"

"Maybe, but I'm not calling him. He's an asshole. He was rude when I called him a couple of weeks ago asking about where Ken might be. I don't think he gives a damn anyway." Then she thought about Katie. She decided to call her to see if she knew anything about it.

Jane called Katie but was unable to reach her that morning. She tried again that afternoon, and she answered. Katie was stunned to hear about Ken and said she never saw him do anything that made her suspect Ken of doing heroin. She knew that Sam sold a lot of weed but never heroin, although it wouldn't surprise her. He had never talked about all the drugs he sold. They agreed that they would get in touch if they heard anything else about this tragedy.

Jane had never tried to call anyone from Ken's family because, as far as she knew, they were all dead or so distant that they never communicated. When his older brother died, he was still living with his mother, and Ken rarely visited them. As far as she knew, his brother had gotten the house when she died but maybe sold it. He probably would have gotten some income from it. At this point, she hadn't known that Ken's mother had left everything to him for some reason.

Jane was experiencing grief far worse now. She couldn't stop thinking about Ken. But it may have been a blessing that she broke up with him if he was that deep into drugs.

"Are you alright," Rita asked?

"No! I'm not okay! Death is a lot to take in."

Then she lowered her head and covered her face with her hands.

She sobbed uncontrollably. Rene sat next to her and held her until she stopped. A night of celebration had changed into a nightmare. A lot of tragedy had happened to both Jane and Ken. Only time would take heal her from the horrible pain.

Now there seemed to be some unanswered questions about Ken. Jane noticed in the article that authorities were looking for a brother, who was a beneficiary of Kelly's life insurance policy. They needed to make funeral arrangements.

"Good luck on that," she thought. Ken's older brother is dead."

After some research, Jane learned that Kelly's body had been moved from El Paso to Albuquerque and was at French Mortuary. Someone had to have arranged it. She also knew that he would be buried at Gate of Heaven Cemetery, a local cemetery, the following day. She considered going to his funeral but was undecided because she wasn't sure she could handle it. She couldn't bear to think about it right now, so she would have to decide later. But more than that, she was tormented about the drugs. She couldn't accept a heroin overdose. It didn't smell right.

Chapter 7

I contacted the New Mexico DMV, and they had a record of my driver's license. I was very excited. It said, Kenneth Joseph Garrity. More importantly, there was an address. My address was a house on 450 Mitchell Dr., Bosque Farms, in New Mexico, almost 20 miles south of Albuquerque. Their records also listed my phone number. I called the number, and it just rang. There was no messaging system in place, so I decided to see if Reverend Myers would give me a ride to my property.

The DMV also had a record of a car registered in my name. It was a 2014 Mazda sedan. The license plate number was FZY 1945. I felt a lot more encouraged than at any other time since my accident. With my new driver's license, I wouldn't need to depend on others to get around, so I decided to get my license as the priority.

I took the bus to the nearest MVD later that day. When I went to get my license renewed, they refused me. I didn't have proof of who I was, so I had to go back to Reverend Myers' house to get my birth certificate. It made me appreciate that Officer Taylor had obtained it and given it to me. But when I returned, they asked for a second form of identification and residency. I argued with the manager and explained my situation and that no one from there told me I needed a second form of ID. He refused to give in, so I called Officer Taylor, and he agreed to verify my fingerprints and vouch for me. But he said he couldn't do it until the following day.

After producing my birth certificate, the next day, Jim vouched for me, and the manager agreed to provide my new driver's license. I was relieved and excited when I left. Jim offered to give me a ride back to the shelter, so that made things easier.

"Finally, I have an ID, and I can drive."

Jim warned that the lab hadn't confirmed that Kelly's overdose was self-administered. I asked if he had time to give me a ride to my address in Bosque Farms instead of the shelter, and he immediately agreed. He reminded me that it might not be safe to stay there yet.

"I appreciate that, but I have to start getting my life back."

"I know that but be careful."

"I will."

When we arrived at 450 Mitchell Dr., The home appeared to be more than 40 years old. It was a light brown one-story stucco house with a flat roof with a simple porch supported by wooden posts and a one-car garage on the north side. The old off-white garage door paint was peeling and needed some TLC. Some of the stucco finish was cracked and chipped, and I decided it needed a new stucco job. There was a small overgrown lawn in the front yard dotted with dandelions and plain-looking pavers extending to the street curb at the end of his property. Some tumbleweed was starting to grow in different parts of the front yard. The xeriscaped yard had sandy-colored gravel.

I smiled when I spotted my Mazda in the gravel driveway leading to the garage. Giant tumbleweeds surrounded it. A white metal gate was on the north side of the house leading to the back yard, where rust-colored concrete Pavers led from the front porch back to the gate entrance. The small backyard was nothing but sand and tumbleweeds. An old metal chain-linked fence surrounded it.

I looked inside the house through the front window, and it appeared to be clean. I wanted to find the keys to the home and the car.

Jim had left my side and walked around the house, looking inside wherever the horizontal blinds provided a view inside. There were no signs of forced entry anywhere, and nothing appeared to have been disturbed during my absence.

I laughed to myself when I noticed a rock next to the door stoop, I thought about looking under it for a key. Indeed, I knew burglars would look there first when trying to break in. When I turned the rock over, I shook my head and moaned, "Damn... stupid me!" There was the key. But my disgust quickly changed to excitement as I held the key in the air so Jim could see it. He smiled, signaled for me to wait, and then urged me to let him go in first. Jim drew his weapon and started towards the front entrance. When he opened the door, the smell of rotten food rushed out, causing us to gasp. I propped the storm door open to let in some fresh air and immediately opened the windows in the house as Jim carefully went from room to room, inspecting all possible hiding places. We met in the living room, and Jim assured me there was no evidence that anyone had been there.

The three-bedroom house included a floor plan that was approximately 1500 square feet. It was pretty clean, and the floor was covered with a tan carpet throughout. It was apparent the carpet needed cleaning, but that would have to wait. There was cheap white linoleum in the kitchen and bathrooms, with green abstract patterns. The walls were painted off-white, and all the rooms were completely furnished with old but clean furniture. There was a living room, dining room, small kitchen, and a hallway with two bedrooms and a bathroom on one side. There was a master bedroom with its bathroom on the other side. The bathroom was small and only had a shower stall, toilet, and sink. Next to the back door was a small laundry room with an off-white washer and dryer in the kitchen next to the back door. I could see the house's back door in the kitchen, leading to a small covered cement patio.

From the looks of the house, I hadn't lived there for very long. It looked basic but neat. When I entered the kitchen, the smell of rotten food grew more robust and was coming from the refrigerator. The electric company had shut off the power.

When I opened the door, I had to fight the gag reflex. There were rotten pork chops and a quart of sour milk. Luckily there wasn't much else in there. Without electricity, the food had spoiled. A baseball bat with part of the handle sawed off, and wrapped in duct tape was leaning up against the counter next to the refrigerator. It looked like it was there for self-defense. Seeing it gave me an odd sensation. The bat seemed to carry some significance to me. I couldn't place what it meant. I quickly shut the refrigerator door and moved to the living room. The beige carpeted living room had an excellent couch, easy chair, coffee table, two lamps on dark varnished pine tables, and a 50" Hisense widescreen TV with a cheap Panasonic surround sound system. There were four nicely framed paintings on the wall. When I took a closer look, I saw my name on them and realized that I must have painted them. They ranged from landscapes to portraits.

When I visited the bedrooms, I found that one had been converted to an office with a desktop computer on a cheap wooden desk with an old beige metal file cabinet next to it. It had scratches, and some of the paint had chipped off. A computer and printer were on top of a small desk but I couldn't stop looking at two nylon-stringed classical guitars leaning against one wall and three guitar cases on the opposite wall. I checked them one by one, strumming them like it was the first time. I found a steel-stringed Martin acoustic guitar and strummed it too. It sounded like it was out of tune, and the sound was unpleasant.

Jim continued to look around the house too. In one of the corners was an empty walnut varnished easel with three blank canvas boards behind it. It looked like a typical home for a bachelor with little decorations aside from the paintings.

In the closet, I found clean clothes, shoes, and five shoeboxes filled with art supplies. There were also two cameras. One was an old Minolta 35 mm with a zoom lens, and the other was a cannon digital camera and a zoom lens. I checked the Minolta and accidentally exposed the film. Jim and I found no pictures on the digital camera.

I couldn't log into the computer at first because I couldn't remember the ID or password, so I looked through the desk drawers and found a spiral notebook with the word "Passwords" on it. I shook my head in disbelief.

"This is a classic example of stupid luck and contradicts the purpose of having secret passwords."

We stayed until I got the gas and electric companies to come and turn on the power. They agreed for me to pay the bills later in the day. Once they restored the power and left, I returned to the computer and started looking through the notebook with the passwords.

Jim stayed back and waited for me to access the computer.

There were many passwords, so it took a few minutes to find the ones I needed. I was eventually able to log into the computer and eventually into my Wells Fargo bank account. There were a lot of documents in files on the desktop of the computer screen as well. I invited Jim to look as I went through each of the websites.

By now, I was tired and decided I would go through all of the digital information later that day. Jim concluded that he was no longer needed and asked if I wanted a ride back to Reverend Myers' house. I declined the offer and told him that I would stay there and try to find my car keys, and if I couldn't, I would call a locksmith. Before Jim left, he tried to convince me to come back to Reverend Myers' house, but I refused. He reminded me to call if I saw or heard anything unusual.

Luckily, I found a spare set of car keys in the nightstand drawer next to my bed. It was a relief.

"Hey Jim, I found a set of car keys. I'm going to check to see if it'll start."

"Sounds like a good idea. If it doesn't, I'll give you a boost."

Surprisingly, the Mazda started after a few tries. I turned on the inside lights to inspect the vehicle and found my registration and proof of insurance. I looked at the mileage, and there were 91,000 miles on it. The motor sounded good, and the breaks felt right. The knowledge that I had transportation made me feel much more secure.

After Jim left, I went to the closest bank and applied for a new debit card and received some blank checks with my name and address on them. They said I would receive a new card within five to seven days. I also took $200.00 of cash out.

After leaving the bank, I called the utility providers again and made some payments through the Wells Fargo bill pay system. Surprisingly, they agreed to overlook the delay in receiving the payments after I explained my circumstances.

I spent the rest of the day cleaning out the refrigerator and sanitizing it. With all the windows open, the smells of decay escaped the house. Things seemed to be back to normal.

I was tired from the drive and activity but couldn't rest. I had to learn more. There was old mail stacked on the desk, and I started emptying the contents from the real estate company that had sold me the house. Next to it was a Wells Fargo Bank statement and several other official documents related to my property. I spent hours going through all of the paperwork. When my mother died, she had left me the house which she had paid off, and I had sold it. She had also left me a portion of her life insurance that amounted to $40,000.

I was able to buy my house with the money earned from the sale of my mother's property. It looked like I had made some intelligent decisions.

My bank statement showed $2,000 in the checking account and $20,000 in his savings account. That was far better than I ever imagined it would be. I felt relieved. I was no longer homeless and had a lot of financial resources. My mailbox was at the front curb and was an old post-mounted type with a flag mechanism on the side to alert the postal employee when I had mail going out. I opened it and found it completely stuffed with mail. When I inspected it, 90% were for marketing and advertising, and the other 10% were bills.

The cable company was just as understanding as my utility companies when I told them my story. They were happy they hadn't lost my business and ended up giving me a cheaper plan with more TV stations and faster internet speed. There was no evidence that I had a steady income or employment. I must have been living off my mother's life insurance policy. I found receipts for a modest number of sales for some of my paintings, though. The most I had earned was $500 for a pen and ink drawing of old, dilapidated houses from the mining era in Madrid, New Mexico.

They were urging me to make arrangements for Kelly's funeral. It would cost $8,000. But there was no evidence that he had life insurance. I was surprised to learn that Kelly's lifestyle wasn't focused on that type of future planning. I decided to pay for it with the money left to me by my mother. I figured she would approve and felt lucky to have a solution.

By the time I went through all of the financial documents, it was 3:00 in the morning. I had the bank change my account number since my wallet and credit cards were gone. I had fallen asleep hunched over the computer desk but woke up at 9:00 am from a phone call from Reverend Myers, who was doing a welfare check. I gave him a summary of what I had learned, and he seemed excited for me. I told him I would keep him informed as I learned new information.

My back was sore from sleeping in an awkward position, so I did some stretches to loosen up. The windows were still open, and so was the front door. It was in the middle of the summer now, and the cross breeze from the open windows had cooled and freshened the house. But I shivered when I thought about the possibility of someone just walking in and killing me if they had wanted. I closed and locked the doors and windows and found some coffee in the kitchen. I brewed a cup from a French coffee press that I found in the cabinet above the sink.

I contacted French Mortuary and agreed to pay for Kelly's funeral and bought a small headstone for an additional $900.00, which took over half of my savings account. Oddly, paying for the funeral made me feel some connection to the twin brother I never knew. Even though I didn't know him, I still felt a loss and sadness.

I then walked to the car with the cup of coffee still in hand, but when I tried to start the vehicle, the battery was dead. I had left the inside lights on, and it had drained the battery. I felt stupid.

I walked to my next-door neighbor's house, and a man came to the door. He had no idea who I was but was willing to give me a jump start. His name was George Tafoya. He appeared to be between his early to mid-fifties, was overweight, and his T-Shirt soiled and had holes in it. He was wearing brown leather sandals and dirty old pair of blue jeans that were frayed on the knees. His balding hair was uncombed, and it appeared he had just gotten out of bed. His hands were worn, and the skin on his fingers was cracked.

"What kind of work do you do?" I asked.

"I work in construction and am a tile setter by trade. It's hard work but a good living. You?

"I'm employed at a homeless shelter center for now."

"That must be interesting work... I know I couldn't do it with all that filth!"

"It has a rewarding side."

"Go get 'em," He laughed.

He said that he had seen the car at this address but hadn't seen anyone come and go, so he thought the owner might have been out of town on a long trip. George went back to his house and returned with his 2006 Silver four-door Toyota Tacoma and parked it facing the front of my car. We connected the two batteries, and after a few tries, it started. I smiled and nodded when I heard the quiet engine hum evenly. I decided to let it run for about 30 minutes to recharge the battery and thanked George, and he waved as he drove back into his driveway.

By now, my thoughts had shifted to Kelly. I some help with the arrangements. I contacted Reverend Myers and Jim. I told them about my plans to go to El Paso to finish making arrangements for my brother's funeral. Both urged me to call them when I arrived to let them know I was safe. Reverend Myers asked if I needed for him to go with me, but I declined his offer. I asked him to help me with French Mortuary and told him I was paying for the funeral and headstone.

"That says a lot about you, my friend," Reverend Myers said.

I didn't respond, but it made me think more positively about my character.

The following day the bank opened at 9:00 am so I went as soon as it opened. I withdrew $300.00 from the account for the trip on Monday morning.

Chapter 8

On Monday morning, I drove to a Speedway gas station on highway 47 and filled my car with gas. I had packed lunch with a thermos I found in my vehicle. I cleaned it and filled it with fresh coffee for the trip, set my Google map for the morgue in El Paso, and was on my way. I texted Jim just before I left, and he reminded me to text him again once I had arrived in El Paso.

At 8:00 am I went straight down I-25 without stopping until El Paso and soon after I arrived, made arrangements for a funeral in Albuquerque. The medical examiner, Shirley Winston, a middle-aged heavy-set woman with gray hair and steel-rimmed glasses, met with me. She had done the autopsy, and the local police were satisfied with her conclusions. She said the bruises on his body indicated that he had been beaten, and she was listing the death as a homicide. She noted that the actual cause of death was a lethal dose of heroin, which had appeared to have been forced on him.

I had informed the mortuary staff in Albuquerque before I left that I would attempt to bury him in a Catholic Cemetery. With the help of Reverend Myers, I had made arrangements, including a headstone, and Kelly's body would be transported in an unidentified hearse to French Mortuary in Albuquerque. He would be laid in state for one day only. I was lucky enough to get his obituary in the Albuquerque Journal in advance of the funeral.

It all seemed like a whirlwind because I hadn't had much time to plan. It was like I was on autopilot, going through the motions. It was tough because my memory hadn't returned, despite all the information overload. Nothing about my past life as it related to Kelly seemed recognizable. I just took action as they came up.

Some things were starting to feel familiar, though. On my drive to El Paso, I-25 south had seemed very familiar, especially when I passed Elephant Butte Lake near Truth or Consequences.

During some of my calls to Reverend Meyers, I had trouble describing the situation without losing control of my emotions. Reverend Myers detected both uncertainty and sadness in my voice, and he kept asking if I was okay.

Jim said that he would contact law enforcement in El Paso to let them know I was there and not be surprised to see a duplicate of Kelly. He said he would try to get more information on my brother's death and brief them on my condition so they wouldn't expect much information from me.

It had been more than a month since my tragic attack, and at 3:00 pm, I was in El Paso, standing in front of the morgue on Alberta Ave and getting ready to view a deceased brother that I didn't know or remember. After about a 15-minute wait, I viewed the body and was surprised that I was feeling an overwhelming sense of grief and despair despite the probability that he and I hadn't ever met. Of course, it felt like I was looking at a dead me. The medical examiner noticed my reaction and asked if I wanted to leave the room. I agreed as I wiped tears from my eyes.

I contacted the mortuary in Albuquerque and told them when the body would arrive. I filled out the paperwork and left the morgue feeling the injustice that had occurred and was angry. But I didn't want to stay a minute longer in El Paso, so I left for Albuquerque as quickly as possible. I contacted Reverend Myers and Jim so they would know I was on the way back.

On the way back to Albuquerque, I found myself struggling to look for things that would jog my memory. It seemed like the harder I tried, the more chaotic everything got. I decided to drive straight home and then do as much research as possible to learn more about my brother and our past.

Everything I had learned so far was beneficial and had I was relieved because there was no new lousy information. I had already obtained a lot of history and had a strong sense of what I needed to do to stabilize my circumstances. But it had been an emotional train wreck, and I was exhausted.

By the time I had gotten back to Albuquerque at 9:00 pm, I had called Reverend Myers and Jim to let them know I had arrived safely. By 9:30 pm, I was already dozing off when Reverend Myers called to make sure I was okay. I briefly covered what I did in El Paso and what I wanted to do when the body arrived. Reverend Myers offered to handle all the arrangements in Albuquerque so I wouldn't have to add that to all my troubles. I thanked him, and within minutes of hanging up, I fell fast asleep and didn't wake up until 6:00 am the following day. Still groggy, I went to the kitchen and found the coffee and French coffee press. I rinsed it out and brewed enough for two cups. I found some powdered non-dairy creamer in one of the cabinets and dumped two heaping teaspoons into the cup. Luckily, the refrigerator was clean and didn't smell anymore. There was some ice in the freezer and a six-pack of Coke Zero. I decided I would go grocery shopping sometime later.

"This refrigerator is pathetic," I thought.

I went to the small laundry room next to the kitchen and checked the washer and dryer. A small built-in ironing board could double for folding clothes and a rod just above the dryer to hang shirts. On the top of the washer was a half-full container of Tide detergent with a small bottle of Clorox bleach next to it. An iron with the cord neatly tied with a Velcro strap was the only other item in the cabinet. From the looks of it, I must have been a fairly neat person. But there wasn't enough there to give it a personal touch.

I grabbed my cup of coffee, sat on the couch in the living room, and watched the news while I sipped. I loved both the smell and taste of freshly brewed coffee. As I got closer to the bottom of the cup, I was already thinking about another one. I could feel the energy from the caffeine.

Nothing was exciting on the TV. It seemed that unless there was news about me, I just wasn't interested. I was consumed with regaining my memory, and if it slowed my recovery, I would have to endure it. My approach wouldn't change. But I was still tired from my trip to El Paso. The drive had been long, and the anxiety and grief had taken their toll.

I revisited the kitchen, poured another cup of coffee, and rechecked the cabinets to see if there was anything there that could curb my hunger. I found some molded bread and threw it in the trash. I also found some peanut butter and stale crackers, so that was breakfast. It tasted like peanut butter on cardboard.

After about 30 minutes, I decided to start researching, so I went back to my home office and sat in front of the computer.

Once I logged into my bank account, I studied it closely. I noticed that I had a debit card that I used for everything from $200 to $2.00. All transactions had stopped on the day I ended up in the mountains.

I called the bank and asked for a rush on the new card, but the bank was too big, and I was too small. The steps would take at least a week. I got excited because I suddenly remembered the PIN for the card. It was somewhat small but enormous to me. I also vaguely remembered purchasing hiking boots but couldn't remember from where I had bought them. I hurried back on the wheels of the office chair, slowly stood up, and stretched. I went back to the closet in the master bedroom, and to my delight, the boots were neatly arranged on the floor of the closet, and precisely the way I remembered them. There was a definite sense of Deja Vu. I started wondering why I wasn't wearing those boots when I went to the mountains. I wasn't dressed at all for the mountains when I was there. But my trip to the mountains was not planned by me.

At 10:00 am, Jim visited me. First, he checked outside of the house and walked around the property. I also showed him some of the personal documents I had found. We compared notes. Jim shared that the vehicle in the mountains had no identifying markers. He believed that it had been stolen and carefully altered in a chop shop. Someone had removed all identifiers from the vehicle. Albuquerque was well known for its car thefts and the black market.

Further, if it had been stolen, there were no reports on file for that make, model, and year recently. It was discouraging. Then Jim dropped a bomb.

"Your brother had been arrested in the past month for drug possession and trafficking heroin, which is a felony that can bring a lot of prison time. He chose to inform law enforcement of some top-level Cartel members who supplied him as part of a plea deal. It would have reduced the crime and penalty, leaving him 18 months in prison instead of several years. It would have also forced him to be a part of the witness protection system. He was out on bail when someone killed him despite being moved to a secret location. It seems obvious the Cartel did it. The word was that he was running his mouth while in jail, and it got back to the wrong people."

The news was alarming. I slumped in a dining room chair and shook my head.

"It's all like a bad dream."

"Are you going to be okay?" Jim asked.

"Of course not. How could I be okay?"

After Jim gave me some of the more minor details, I told him that I would be going through my computer and documents and would call him if I found something that might be helpful. It was going to take some time to be thorough. Right now, my primary interest was to find something that might jog my memory. I was frustrated that I hadn't made more progress yet thankful that I had learned a great deal from my brother's unfortunate death. I decided that once my memory returned, I would use all of my energy to find out why my brother had started using drugs. I wondered if I had already known something about it. If so, I just had to find where it was hiding in my brain.

I decided to take a break to let my mind wander for a while. I was putting too much pressure again. I moved a green and white webbed lawn chair from my back porch to the front and sat with my eyes closed. As my body slowly relaxed, I focused my senses on the sounds of birds chattering from the surrounding trees, which gradually took me back to when I was lost in the mountains. I could also hear the wind blowing through the trees, dogs barking in the distance, and a lawnmower a few houses down. My nose detected the pleasant scent of eggs and bacon cooking for either a late breakfast or brunch. Faint sounds of Mexican music were floating in the wind and gradually caused me to drift into a light sleep. It was the kind of sleep where a person can still hear the background noises.

Eventually, my thoughts started wandering, seemingly in rhythm with the wind. My mind finally stumbled onto the chaotic sequence of events of the night I found myself being manhandled. I was being kicked and beaten on the ground, and my hands were tied. I was jerking and screaming and felt the pain rushing through my head. There was a silhouette of three men, and they were dragging me to the ground. I was thrown into the back seat of a vehicle and punched in the head. It was terrifying, and I felt trapped. I struggled to wake up but was unable to escape the nightmare. It was like I was paralyzed and trapped in a horror movie. When I finally wrenched my eyes open and broke from the nightmare, I was sweating and gasping for air. I knew it had to have been the memory of what happened that awful night. But there were still a lot of unanswered questions about it? The most obvious were who and why?

After I was fully awake and had regained my composure, I went back into the house. I decided to write down what happened in the dream in as much detail as possible so I wouldn't forget any of it. From that moment on, I started journaling everything I could remember to keep track of whatever surfaced from my memory. It all seemed like a giant puzzle with a lot of missing pieces. But more and more were starting to appear. Some of the memories were fragmented, and I couldn't make sense of them, but I put them in writing anyway. After I was satisfied with the accuracy of the information, I called Jim and was surprised that he answered because I knew he was busy. I gave the account of my dream, and he thanked me for the information. He encouraged me to keep writing things down. He also reminded me that it would be smart for me to share this information with the Dr. who was treating me. He said my Dr. might have some ideas on how to use the information to help him recover faster. I agreed but had decided to stop the treatment. It just didn't seem helpful right now.

I continued to look at documents and computer files until my eyes couldn't focus anymore. But the more I looked, the more I learned about myself. The person I was reading about still seemed like someone else.

I felt relieved that there was still no evidence of any illegal activity by me. Now and then, something would catch my attention and would seem familiar. It was encouraging. Each time it happened, I described it in my journal. I kept reading through all of the entries several times. It helped with capturing familiar persons, places, and times. Most importantly, I felt as if I was making progress.

Later that day, I made a list of groceries to restock my cabinets. I went to the nearby Albertsons and purchased $150.00 of groceries. When I returned home and put it all away, I felt good because, for now, I didn't need to go anywhere but work and back home again. I had everything I needed and ultimately felt secure for now.

Chapter 9

On the day of Kelly's funeral, I went into the mortuary and viewed Kelly's body before signing the guest book. His body had an ashy appearance and was stone cold. Reverend Myers and Jim came about thirty minutes after I got there. There were some men from Reverend Myers' congregation who had agreed to join me as pallbearers and others who just decided to attend to honor a passing life. No other persons were there, and no one else had signed in as guests. I was hoping I might meet a visitor who knew him or me. The mortician told me that two Hispanic men had shown up and viewed Kelly's body very early that morning. But they hadn't signed the guestbook, even after he had reminded them. He had never seen them before, and they didn't stay long. I asked him to describe the two men, but he couldn't remember much about them because they were evasive and avoided eye contact. I took a mental note because it seemed odd.

Reverend Myers had scheduled a funeral service at the church. When we lifted the casket onto the Hearse, I was surprised at the weight. It was a lot heavier than I had imagined. When we arrived at the church, I saw stained glass windows on each side depicting Christ at different stages of his life. The interior had a simple design with pews facing a podium and a communion table with a small cross on it. There was a much bigger cross on the wall behind it.

I noticed many people in attendance and was sure that they had come at the request of Reverend Myers. It was a nice gesture, and I appreciated it. He had a very moving eulogy, reminding everyone that every soul deserved honor when laid to rest, and Kelly was forever at peace.

I hoped that fond memories of a happy past with my brother would replace all of this sorrow once my memory returned. If I never met him, then my only memory would be the tragedy and sight of his dead body.

All the pallbearers rode in one of the limousines and followed the hearse towards the cemetery. We were escorted slowly by law enforcement motorcycles to Gate of Heaven Cemetery. Once the casket was placed over the freshly dug grave, Reverend Myers presented a short eulogy. He prayed for those who might have known him and emphasized the importance of accepting the grief and working through it.

Jim, Reverend Myers, some parishioners, and I were the only ones in attendance. I kept looking around to see if anyone else might show up, but no one did. It suddenly dawned on me that there was a good chance that no one in attendance knew my brother.

"When a person dies, a lot of people should show up to honor the passing of his or her life," I thought. I had heard that the memory of a person after death only lasts two generations. It seemed that Kelly's memory wouldn't even last one.

After we lowered the coffin into the ground, Jim and Reverend Myers gave their condolences and asked me what I had planned for the day.

"I think I'll stay awhile and then go home."

"Okay, but if you need anything, call," Reverend Myers said.

Jim nodded his head towards Reverend Myers as made the offer.

"I will, but right now, I need some time alone to think."

When they left, I stood very still with my head bowed and eyes closed next to the open grave for about thirty minutes. I kept thinking about my brother the gravity of the moment. After whispering a few silent prayers, I put my hands into my pockets, focused my eyes on the ground in front of me, and started walking slowly towards my car. I decided to return within a week to bring flowers and give my brother some company. I hoped it might help trigger memories about us too. There were quite a few unanswered questions, and I desperately needed more information to unravel this bizarre situation.

As I approached my car, I looked up and was startled when a beautiful young woman with red hair and freckles came towards me. Her skin was pale from fright as she stared at me in disbelief. She looked as if she saw a ghost. She somehow looked familiar.

"Ken is that you," she asked in a trembling voice with tears running down her face.

When I heard her voice, I was both surprised and confused. "But who are you?"

"It's Jane!" she exclaimed as her face completely turned white. "You look like you've seen a ghost," I said.

"I think I have," she answered in a trembling voice.

After a few moments, I guessed that Jane must have known my brother and said, "You must have known my brother Kelly. We were identical twins."

"No! I know you, Ken, and I recognized your car, but I'm still confused. And by the way, you didn't tell me you had a twin!"

I panicked because she had startled me, and I was confused. After a few awkward moments, I leaned towards her. I said, "I'm sorry, I'm at a disadvantage because I was in an automobile accident over a month ago, and I'm still trying to recover my memory. Who are you, and how do I know you?"

Jane's expression turned from shock to anger. She bit her lower lip, and the anger on her face changed to hurt as she answered, "I guess I had that coming. I know you think I was faking the amnesia after my accident."

I tilted my head in total bewilderment. "What are you talking about?"

"Yeah, right!"

"No! Honestly, I don't remember who you are. I wish I did."

"Okay, I see what 's happening here! I knew it was a mistake coming here!"

She started running at a slow pace towards her car.

I quickly followed her. "No! No, seriously! What's your last name?"

"Yeah, right!" she yelled as she quickened her pace. She wasn't looking back as she got closer to her car.

I ran faster, eventually got ahead of her, and blocked her path. I reached out and touched her shoulder to stop her forward movement. I was well aware that this woman had known me somehow and could help me remember my past. But I pulled my hand away, fearful that she might scream.

"Ma'am, I can prove what happened to me. You can talk to Reverend Myers, who got me into his Shelter, and the sheriff's deputy, who took the police report on my accident. They'll verify everything I've told you. This has been an awful time for me, and if you do know me, I need your help to get my life back. I spent two days in the hospital and didn't know anyone. I'm just now starting to find out information about me. I just recently learned my identity because of my brother's death. I don't even remember him. If you leave, I might lose everything!"

Jane studied my desperate expression and suddenly turned towards me. She folded her arms across her breasts and took a deep breath.

"So, you really don't know my name is Jane Connors?"

"No, I don't. I really don't, but I wish I did!"

Jane's doubt seemed to change from suspicion to curiosity. For a few moments, she was silent and appeared to be trying to decide what to do next.

"So, what's this about your amnesia?" I asked.

"Well, first, I would like to take you up on your offer and talk to the two men you mentioned, not just because I want to believe you, but so I can get their story." Jane stared at me as she carefully chose her words. I thought she was starting to believe me.

"I think maybe I can help them and you if what you are telling me is the truth."

Despite my convincing story, Jane didn't seem sold on my account, but I was convinced that once she spoke to Reverend Myers and Jim, that would all change.

The dilemma went in both directions; I had a right to be wary of her too, but she seemed sincere in the way she had reacted.

"I'm sure you'll believe me when you talk to them.

"We'll see."

I then suggested we should have a meeting with Reverend Myers and Officer Taylor as quickly as possible. She agreed, and we exchanged phone numbers.

I was confident that we could all meet soon because my new friends would seize the opportunity to put more puzzle pieces together.

When I contacted Jim, he was excited to hear the news. He reminded me that Jane had to have a lot of history that could help me regain my memory and maybe provide leads on the crime against me. He agreed to meet as soon as I could arrange it.

When I contacted Reverend Myers, he was jubilant. He suggested that we all try to meet at the Shelter to talk the very next day. The Shelter would be a neutral place, more comfortable and safer for everyone. I needed to be there that day anyway because some of the mayor's staff were touring the Shelter. I had agreed to help with the tour. Reverend Myers suggested that we all sit and eat a meal together while discussing my current situation and then getting Jane to share everything she knew. We all agreed to meet the following day at 5:30 pm if Jane could make it.

When I contacted Jane, she agreed to meet us at the Shelter. Then she started crying.

"What's the matter?" I pleaded.

"I'm just happy you're still alive."

"Me too."

After we hung up, I was more confident that she was starting to believe me.

The next day Jane met me right on time at the Shelter. Reverend Myers was there, but Jim hadn't arrived yet. I introduced Jane to Reverend Myers as soon as we walked through the entrance. A volunteer from the Shelter brought us some iced tea while we waited for Jim.

Most of the conversation was between Jane and Reverend Myers. "So, where did you meet Ken?"

"I met him at a place in Corrales where he was singing and playing his guitar."

Reverend Myers looked at me approvingly and said, "So you are a musician."

I shrugged my shoulders and shook my head as Jim entered the shelter. We all stood and greeted him. He was in full uniform because he was still on his shift. After he sat down, we started talking about my situation immediately. Reverend Myers explained how Ken had come to the shelter and the severe head injuries I had suffered. He explained how he and Officer Taylor had agreed to help me the way they had because of the potential danger. Jane seemed very concerned about my injuries, but especially the threat.

We drank tea, ate some hamburgers and talked for almost two hours. Jane told us a lot about my history with her when we were a couple. After listening to Jane's story and how our relationship ended, I now realized why she had reacted the way she did at the cemetery. It also explained why I was feeling a connection with her. She hadn't pulled any punches when she told about our break-ups, and I understood why on the first one. But she said the second break-up was because I was pressuring her, and she couldn't handle it because of the trauma she had experienced. She was overwhelmed, and I wouldn't or couldn't give her the space to heal as she needed. She also made it clear that she had been questioning her decision to break up. She looked right into my eyes when she said it. It made me wonder how it must have been for me.

Jim asked her a lot of questions about her associations. She told them about Sam and Katie and that they weren't communicating much anymore. He seemed interested in Sam and wanted to know how he might contact him, but Jane couldn't help. She said she would ask Katie. The last time she had spoken to her, Katie didn't know where he was anymore and didn't want to know.

Jim told Jane that he was probably going to need to talk to her again in the future. He thought she might be able to help solve the apparent crime against me. It made me uncomfortable when Jim asked her questions about my past and if I did drugs or had gotten into any trouble. I knew he had to ask those questions, and even though I was afraid, I wanted to know too. It was a relief to hear Jane say that she knew of no past legal problems about me.

After we all finished talking about our past and our mutual friends, Jim asked me if I had been seeing any of the Doctors for guidance to help get my memory back. I told him I really hadn't had the time with everything going on but would contact him as soon as possible.

Since it was Friday, I decided to try the following Monday. Jane and her parents went to Elephant Butte Lake in southern New Mexico. They had planned to go water skiing and had reserved a campsite. She surprised me when she said I had gone with them once. She told me my efforts to ski were a disaster, but she was happy that I had tried.

I talked to Jane on the phone a couple of times over the weekend while she was at the lake. We agreed to get together again on Monday evening after work. We texted a lot during the weekend, asking and answering questions, and I wanted to spend more time with her. She was my path to the past, and I also liked being around her. The attraction was more than looks and personality. It was both chemical, spiritual.

Chapter 10

I was able to get an appointment with Dr. Lewis at the Presbyterian Rust Medical Center for the following Monday morning, and it was an excellent way to start the week. Dr. Lewis examined me and asked several questions, testing my every response. He referred me to a specialist named Brad Nicholson, who specialized in brain injury patients. He was able to get me an appointment for later that afternoon. His office was in the same building. Dr. Lewis had sent my CAT scan information to Dr. Nicholson and assured me that he had a good reputation and would help me develop a good rehabilitation plan.

Dr. Nicholson was an older man with white hair, and his midriff was over his belt. He had a new England accent and wore green tortious shell-framed reading glasses with straps hanging around his neck.

After asking me questions about any symptoms like headaches or vision problems, he said my physical recovery was looking good. He asked me to be patient and keep a journal to refer to it when past events started coming back. I told him that I was already using a journal, so he asked me to add everything positive each day. He said doing that would help me maintain optimism. He was very encouraged that I wasn't experiencing headaches or dizziness anymore.

Before we finished, he cautioned that my memory might still take a while to return. However, there were no obvious signs of long-term brain injury. I had sustained enough trauma to make memory recovery slow.

But Dr. Nicholson said he was very confident that my memory would fully return. He said it might come back gradually or all at once. It could last anywhere from days to months, though. He was encouraged about my progress so far. I had already remembered a lot with the help of Jim and Reverend Myers.

Dr. Nicholson suggested that if I continued having trouble with my memory, he would ask Jane to come with me for my next visit. He said he would assign some activities to us to speed up the process.

When I returned home that night and called Jane, I told her about my visit with Dr. Nicholson, and she offered to accompany me to my next appointment if it would help.

After the phone call, I sat on my couch to let my mind wander. It seemed to work when I needed to think, better than anything else. Maybe something from the past would pop up. I tilted my head back, leaning against a soft pillow from my bed, and shifted my body until I felt comfortable. As my thoughts wandered, my feelings kept returning my attention to Jane. I was attracted to her. It wasn't just the conversations either. Other senses, such as smell, voice, and emotional connection, played an even more substantial role in the relationship. I felt something vital and kept feeling like I wanted to hug her to feel her energy. I knew those emotional connections linked to memories from the past. I almost fell asleep but caught myself. I didn't want to oversleep and miss my visit with Jane. I went to my bedroom, grabbed my cell phone, and set the alarm for 5:30 pm. I was supposed to meet with Jane at 7:00 pm.

I eventually drifted into a deep sleep and started dreaming. At first, it was enjoyable. I could see my mother from a small child's eyes. It seemed like random memories trying to return to my consciousness. Then events shifted, and I started dreaming of being beaten and thrown on the ground. Even though I was asleep, I had enough awareness to know that despite the fear it caused, it wasn't happening at that moment. But eventually, I started reliving the terror and felt paralyzed. I struggled to wrench myself away from the dream and finally woke up and jumped out of bed. I paced back and forth until I calmed down.

I then realized that it was only 30 minutes before the alarm was supposed to go off, so I reviewed the dream a couple of times and remembered it vividly. I pulled my journal from the coffee table and wrote everything down in as much detail as I could remember. It was exasperating that I couldn't visualize the faces of any of the attackers in my dreams, but at least I remembered a lot of action. I recognized three of them and that they were stronger than me. They were wearing pullover shirts and jeans with hiking boots.

Before leaving for Jane's apartment, I rubbed some water into my hair, brushed and then combed it. Afterward, I changed to a clean pair of jeans, a button-down, short-sleeved tan leisure shirt, and dark blue tennis shoes from my closet. I found some Yardley cologne in my bathroom medicine cabinet and sprayed some on my chest. It had a delightful scent, and I wanted to impress Jane.

On the way to Jane's apartment, my mind drifted to some of the collateral effects of my recent trauma and memory loss. Some of it was positive. There was a natural tendency to be more reflective. I was beginning to feel calmer about who I thought I might be. I knew that there would be some regrets about certain parts of my past life, but I felt a sense of optimism because of most of what I had learned so far. I was hopeful that once my memory returned, I would be happy. Since the beginning of this nightmare, I had been dreading that there may be something terrible in my past. Some of the anxiety was still there.

I also thought about some other good things about my current circumstances. Because my injury magnified my senses, there was less history in my conscious mind and my experiences with day-to-day events were more focused on the present. When I was outside my home and walking around, I was able to see more, with a hypersensitive sense of smell and hearing. My sense of smell connected some memories, but I still couldn't put it all together. But. I was enjoying the feeling that each experience provided. I appreciated all the different outdoor sounds, including the volume of birds communicating in the trees, especially during the morning hours. I wondered if I had paid any attention to it in my previous life. If so, I hoped I would never take it for granted again. Even the sound of leaves blowing across the ground was magnified.

I knew there was still a lot to do and I couldn't sit around just thinking about it. I still needed to look through all of the papers in my home and continue researching information related to my name.

My thoughts turned to Jane as I neared her apartment building that night. It was in a complex that was three stories high and was named Casa Verdi West. The style was typical southwestern with light green synthetic stucco walls with white trim on the doors and windows. Each apartment had a balcony on the second and third floors and a ground-level porch on the first. Her apartment was on the second floor, with 211 nailed to the wall left of her front door. I found a parking space about fifteen yards from the stairs going to her apartment and checked the time on my smartphone as I approached the building. I was about fifteen minutes late, so my pace quickened. The steel stairs were painted white and had a crisscross see-through pattern forcing me to see to the ground as I climbed. When I stepped onto the long brown wooden walkway leading to apartment 211, the smell of pork ribs coming from one of the apartments filled my nostrils and made me hungry.

When I finally reached her apartment, I suddenly felt nervous because I wanted the visit to be positive, and at that moment, saying the wrong thing could be a real setback. When I knocked on the freshly painted white metal door, I heard footsteps coming quickly on the other side and a small dog barking.

"I guess they allow pets here," I thought. Pavement surrounded the apartments. I wondered how much work it caused for Jane taking him in and out when he had to relieve himself.

"I'm sure she has figured it out," I concluded.

When Jane opened the door, my eyes widened as I scanned her curvy figure. She had the perfect amount of make-up for her fair skin and freckled complexion. Her wavy orange hair fell to both sides of her neck and down her yellow blouse, partially covering her well-shaped breasts. It was evident that she had just finished curling it. She was wearing pale blue jeans that matched her eyes. Her caramel brown sandals exposed the red nail polish on her toes, which matched her fingernails. I couldn't take my eyes off of her.

"Come on in," she said as she grabbed my hand and pulled me inside. She appeared nervous but happy to see me. A little white miniature poodle was continuously barking, partially hiding behind her ankle.

"Don't worry about Bailey. He'll calm down. Believe it or not, he knows you," she laughed. "He's never bitten anyone either."

"What do you do when Bailey has to go to the bathroom?"

"Oh, I have a box with dirt in it on the balcony and has a toy fire hydrant in it. It works like a kitty box," She giggled. "But it's still a lot of work cleaning it every day."

After I was in the apartment, I detected the scent of some meat sauce. It made me very hungry because I hadn't eaten since breakfast. I looked around the room, dominated by a pleasant mixture of earth tones with different brown, rust, and green shades.

"This looks and smells really new."

"It just opened six months ago, and I got lucky to find it, especially since they allow small pets.

Jane took me on a brief tour of the apartment, and every room was neatly organized and spotless. Bailey followed her as if he were tied to her ankles, occasionally jumping up the side of her leg.

The master bedroom's colors were primarily pink and white and filled with stuffed animals. The comforter on the bed was beautiful with white and blue rings and pink flowers. A white bureau dresser with a mirror was opposite the foot of the bed, and there were floral arrangements against the mirror. On each side of the bed were white wooden end tables and white ceramic lamps with pink shades. In the guest room next to it was a twin bed with similar decorations and small office space with a desk, laptop, printer, and phone.

"It looks like a picture from some home decoration magazine."

"Thank you. I am happy with it."

"I can tell that a female lives here with all the stuffed animals and colors," I laughed.

We walked into the living room, which was an open floor plan leading into the dining area. I noticed a small walnut dining room table with four matching chairs. Jane touched my arm and pointed at a painting that was a likeness of Bailey. I studied it and looked back inquisitively at Jane.

"You painted it," she whispered. "Take a closer look."

I moved closer to the painting and immediately spotted the name "K Garrity" scribbled with black paint in the lower right-hand corner. It surprised me. I studied it admiringly for a couple of minutes and felt proud that she had it hanging on her wall. It had a lot of detail and looked professional. When I glanced back at her again, she had a wide grin on her face and smiled mischievously.

"An outstanding artist painted it."

She laughed as she looked in the direction of the kitchen and asked, "Would you like some spaghetti and meatballs?"

"Wow, I haven't eaten since this morning, and I'm starving."

Jane and I ate some salad that she had prepared and then the spaghetti and meatballs. She poured some iced tea and sat it next to my plate. It was delicious. While we ate, we said very little because it was still a little awkward. But we smiled a lot.

After finishing and putting the dishes in the sink, we went into the living room and sat on the sofa. Jane then took the initiative.

"We had some excellent times together. You were always polite and funny, and I loved to hear you sing. Everything seemed perfect until you cheated on me."

"Cheated?"

Jane explained it all again. She reminded me that I had hurt her badly, but she had decided to give me another chance after a while since it hadn't happened before.

"I'm sorry I did that to you. I must be stupid. I wonder what else I've done."

"It was stupid... but I have faith that you won't do it again because the Ken I know is a good person," she said.

I asked a lot more questions about what she knew of my past, and it turned out that she didn't see a lot of the distant past but shared what I had told her when we were together. She had been living with her parents at the time we had broken up. I had stayed a few days at her house with some painful digestive disorder. She said she thought it was probably because of all my recent family losses and anxiety.

We must have gotten very close for her to offer that kind of support. She said that I had never brought up anything about my twin brother. It was as if he hadn't existed. But she had met my mother, and even though she had made Jane uncomfortable, she liked her. She wasn't sure my mother liked her. She told me everything she remembered about my mother and the things she said. It was strange having someone else tell me about my parent as if I never knew her.

Jane stopped talking and looked directly into my eyes. "Does any of this sound familiar to you?"

"No, not at all. It's discouraging."

"Do you remember anything about your twin brother?"

I shook my head. "I wish I did."

"Well, since you never mentioned Kelly during the whole nine months, we were together, you can imagine my confusion and surprise when I found out about him. When I saw his picture, I thought it was you, and I cried. I was so sad."

Jane talked about our mutual friends, Sam and Katie, in great detail. She described some of the things we did together and included what Katie had mentioned regarding Sam's contempt for me.

I found myself repeatedly looking up at the ceiling and sometimes shaking my head because there were so many missing pieces. Sam had snubbed me. He had told everybody he had grown to despise me. A lot had happened, and Sam was no longer with Katie.

"I talk to Katie from time to time. When Sam broke up with her, he was rude to everyone, especially after meeting his new girlfriend, Becky. I never met her, but she sounds just like him."

Suddenly I noticed that her wall clock said 10:00 pm. I pointed and said, "I think I need to get back to my house. I have to go to work at the Shelter tomorrow. I'm thrilled we got to visit, and you are a good cook. You've been very helpful to me and I want to do this again."

"Of course, that would be great!"

When I stood up, Jane approached me and put her arms around my neck. At first, it made me uncomfortable. Part of me wanted to hold her and kiss her, and another part was afraid. But I hugged her anyway. There was a faint odor of a sweet-smelling perfume, and the feel of her soft warm skin against his body which was very pleasant.

She whispered in my ear, "You're wearing the cologne I got you for your birthday."

"Sorry, but I didn't know that. But I'm glad."

She then collapsed into me, and it felt good. When she looked up, I gazed into her translucent blue eyes and said, "I'll text you when I get home." I had an even stronger urge to kiss her but dismissed the idea because I was afraid it would ruin the moment. I slowly let go and started to leave.

As I walked towards the door, I felt her hand hook my elbow, and she forcefully spun me around. She then pulled me towards her and kissed me passionately. At first, I started to pull away but then drew her tightly against my body. I kissed her with more force and caressed her neck. Once we released each other, I stood and stared at her like a love-struck teenager.

"Wow," I sighed.

It was great to feel the close connection, but it seemed almost too soon. There was still something uncomfortable about it. I felt hopeful that we might be getting things back to a better place, whatever that place was. But I wanted more.

When I turned around and walked to the door, my mind was flooded with dopamine. My thoughts were prancing around as I drove from the parking lot onto the road to return home. Parts of our visit were undeniably emotional.

Chapter 11

When Sam Zachery left Katie Harmon for Becky Espinosa, it was an excellent step up for his lifestyle. Becky was someone that had all the right qualities for him. Becky's wealth, education, and refinement were very attractive to him. She was two years older than him and more stable. But Becky was manipulative too. Capitalizing on his ego was easy when she wanted something from him.

Becky wasn't Sam's usual type of girlfriend. He had favored shy nonassertive women who gave him his way and tolerated his wandering eye. Becky was different. She was a stunningly beautiful, assertive woman employed at a high salaried job with a bank and a wealthy family. Becky had long jet-black satin hair and was a tall woman at 5'11", slightly taller than Sam. She had beautiful long sexy legs and was manicured from her regular visits to high-end beauty salons. Her polished red nails and perfect makeup made her beautiful hazel eyes and olive skin present an exotic figure. She dressed in expensive attire that flowed with her self-confident gait.

Becky enjoyed competing with men in business and often celebrated outperforming them. Even though she liked men, she liked the feeling of superiority when she out-achieved them. She chose boyfriends that would enhance her image and had self-confidence. Sam was a perfect fit for her. When past boyfriends had gotten too attached and wanted to get married, they became an annoyance to her. She didn't want to be with a man who was emotionally fragile and dependent. She discarded them like an empty can of beer.

Sam fit perfectly into Becky's social life too. He had a handsome appearance and looked professional when she dressed him up. She added some expensive attire to his wardrobe, and he didn't object. Becky felt that he looked like someone she could keep around for a while. With a bit of coaching, he would make a nice trophy boyfriend. As a bonus, his skills in bed were impressive.

Sam's previous long-time girlfriend, Katie, warned Becky about his past infidelities in a fit of anger. But she already knew. After all, that's how she met him.

After her parting confrontation with Katie, Becky made it clear to Sam that she had a "one-strike and you're out" rule before agreeing to an exclusive relationship. In her case, Becky had always chosen monogamous relationships in the past and ended relationships before starting new ones. She moved on when she got annoyed with a relationship or had spotted a more attractive suitor. She wasn't opposed to an occasional affair with a beautiful female if there were no interesting males around either.

Sam had vowed to make an exclusive commitment to Becky. As in the past, he was sure he could remain faithful, and only time would tell if he could finally follow through. Sam assured her that she was different from anyone he had ever met, and it was evident that he was smitten with her. He was very happy to move in with her when she proposed it to him. She had her own house on the westside of Albuquerque, and it afforded a lavish existence. It was worth over a million dollars. Becky had paid off most of it in the first few years.

Becky's father, Gerald Espinosa, was very wealthy and a ruthless business mogul who had immigrated to the US from Mexico before she was born. He was tall at 6'2" and very fit for 58 years old. Ymelda, his wife of 20 years, had died from breast cancer shortly after Becky was born, and he had taken it hard because she had been so loyal to him. She was an accountant who was talented in finding legal loopholes to help build the Espinosa financial empire. He decided never to remarry out of loyalty to his deceased wife and didn't want to share his wealth with anyone who might try to take what he and his first wife had built. Besides, his wealth attracted beautiful women who stayed until he thought they were getting too serious.

Gerald was in the oil business and had put large sums of money into U.S. political congressional campaigns supporting candidates who stood for big oil and were against renewable energy. He was relentless about protecting his oil empire. He loved his daughter and was always willing to help her get ahead and live a life of luxury. She was like her mother and was a talented, certified accountant. He hoped she would eventually replace his wife in that role.

Becky's home was a 4000 square foot Spanish-style five-bedroom house. The front of the house included a tan stucco-walled courtyard encompassing the front walk and a small outdoor seating area leading to the front entrance. The roof was covered with rust-colored clay Spanish tile. There was a large, well-landscaped backyard for entertainment. A swimming pool and jacuzzi with lawn chairs surrounding it was in the center. The rest of the yard included a small lawn, a self-contained gas barbeque, and eating area in a large, beautifully tiled covered patio. The property was surrounded by tan stucco walls that matched the house. Against the back wall was a small fishpond with a fountain in the center. There were security cameras and a large ATD Security sign in the front xeriscaped yard.

Inside the home were a large living room and dining room connected to a large kitchen area with brown marbleized granite countertops and an island that was perfect for entertaining. It provided a lot more space than she needed but served her image well. The floors were varying colors of rust-colored quarry tile with beautiful Navajo throw rugs. The colors of the stucco-style walls alternated from tan to white. The ceilings had mahogany-stained tongue and groove panels in between traditional vigas. Every bedroom had a bathroom. The design in them was traditional Spanish tile with bright blue, red, and yellow decorative art. Huge southwestern stone fireplaces were central to the living room and den. The furnishings were also southwestern bought from the best stores in Santa Fe. To Sam, it was like a mansion.

It was clear that Becky was the one in charge of Sam and her, and he didn't care. It was a fair trade for a significantly upgraded lifestyle. She had already helped Sam get a job and it was Sam's biggest challenge. He had never really held a steady job. He had gone to school part-time to learn a plumbing trade but hadn't had the ambition to complete it. Becky was determined to change this part of his life. She had found someone who hired him as an apprentice.

Juan Gonzales was one of many clients that Becky had at her bank. Becky had helped Juan qualify for a substantial loan for his plumbing business as requested by her father.

Gerald and Juan had bonded over an incident that happened when he was on vacation in Mexico. When he was leaving a bar one night, a man tried to rob him at gunpoint when he walked towards his vehicle. Juan, who was in the bar, saw the man pull his weapon, rushed out of the bar, and shot the man who died at the scene. Juan wasn't charged for murder because of the circumstances. He and Gerald became nearly inseparable after that. They were a fundamental mismatch because Gerald was always well-dressed and groomed, while Juan was always in dirty work clothes and looked rough. Gerald secretly helped Juan pay off his loan with the bank early to help build his credit. Becky was willing to help because she loved her father and would do anything for him. In the end, she helped Juan with more than just one loan to upgrade his establishment and market his plumbing business.

Now Juan owed her a favor, so Becky set Sam up for an interview, and Juan hired him on the spot, even though he hadn't gotten his plumbing certification yet. Sam understood that he had to get his certificate as a journeyman within a year to keep the job. As a favor to Becky, he was given a handsome salary as an apprentice. But Juan was clear that he wasn't thrilled about Sam and also made it clear that he would fire Sam if he didn't do his part.

Becky's father was more than willing to help his only daughter become successful so he could hand the family business down to her when he retired. He had inherited his fortune from his father, Edwardo Espinosa, who had discovered oil not too far from Mexico City, developed it, and brought his son into the business when he was quite young. Like Gerald, he was a ruthless businessman causing his empire to multiply. As a result, the Espinosa family name had become very influential in Mexico. They had gained some financial influence in the U.S. as well by supporting political figures indirectly. Some believed they had dabbled in illegal activity in Mexico too. But all these accusations were nothing but jealousy, according to Edwardo. There had never been any evidence of criminal activity.

Becky told her father she was going with Sam, and he wasn't impressed. Sam was not Hispanic, so Gerald didn't trust him. Secondly, he was worried about Sam's lack of ambition and business experience, which could embarrass him and his daughter. Gerald was angered when he found out she had helped Sam get a job as an apprentice for Juan. He told her she had made a big mistake. But Becky didn't back down and told him that Sam was just rough around the edges and would prove him wrong. Gerald was still unimpressed.

Even though Sam had seemed to have won the lottery with Becky, he was feeling pressure like never before. His craving for money had gotten the best of him. He no longer felt like he had the freedom that he had enjoyed before. He wasn't sure he could handle the responsibility and the growing dark side of Juan in his business associations.

"Just look at all the compromises," he thought. "How much was it worth?"

In the relatively short time, he had been working at his new job, there was growing tension in his relationship with Juan. He wasn't just doing the plumbing jobs. Juan pressured him to sell illegal drugs on the side, and he was so aggressive Sam went along even though he knew it was going to worsen. He wasn't telling Becky about it because Juan had made it clear that he would regret it if he told anyone outside the shop. Sam didn't know what she would do if she found out. Becky knew he did drugs and even sold them on a small scale, but they had never discussed how much he was doing now. It didn't appear that she knew about the seamy side of Juan because he was always very polite to her. He was afraid Becky would break up with him if she knew. Sam knew he had crossed a line engaging in drug trafficking, and he felt trapped.

All of Sam's recent conduct was catching up to him rapidly, and he was searching for an escape but instead kept digging himself into a deeper hole. His life was collapsing around him.

Juan's business was doing very well and was expanding. Even with his growing business, Juan's means didn't quite seem to match his lifestyle. He had a beautiful new fully loaded 2019 sapphire blue Mercedes, a new 2018 Cadillac, and a 2019 GMC pick-up truck. The shop had three separate work areas with a private office in the back and equipment with tools for employees to use for repairing and install plumbing, heating, and air conditioning. All of the equipment was state of the art. Customers could purchase parts in the front at the cash register with debit and credit card slides. Next to the front door were more shelves with high-end tools and features that customers could grab and purchase as soon as they walked in the door.

Behind the building was a fenced-in parking lot were three white Dodge vans. They had magnetic placards on the doors donned with "Juan's Plumbing and Heating" on the side, thoroughly equipped for repair equipment, and stocked with parts needed to do service calls.

At first, Juan had been easier to work for because even though he was sometimes distant, he was friendly and helpful to Sam and other employees when they asked questions. He gave a lot of cash bonuses to some of his employees when they finished work early. Juan paid cash so there wouldn't be any taxes. He always had a lot of weed and openly shared it when there was something to celebrate, like scoring a big job. He often sat and passed a joint back and forth with employees laughing about how stupid some of the customers were. Sam was the only non-Hispanic working for him. In the beginning, Juan lured Sam by giving him a pound of weed here and there, so he could break them down into one-ounce baggies to sell to his friends. Juan took fifty percent of the take. Sometimes he would let Sam sample weed laced with heroin or coke and eventually convinced him to smoke opium. Juan made it clear that he could supply any drug Sam wanted to try.

It didn't take long before Juan gave Sam an ultimatum to go with some of his gangster friends to muscle someone who had crossed him. What he had done for Juan was still haunting him, not only because it was a serious crime but because Juan would forever have leverage on him. Juan started sending him on more assignments with some of his friends that could get them all locked up in prison for years. He had participated enough so that leaving Juan's sideshow would be dangerous. One of his assignments involved minor participation in murdering someone who was stealing drugs from Juan. But he could still be convicted of murder as an accessory. He couldn't get it out of his head. Worse, Sam knew Juan disliked him and that it wouldn't take much for him to be on the receiving end of the violence.

Juan knew he would have to lure Sam into engaging in the illegal side of his business to keep him quiet because sooner or later, he would be a witness to some of it. At first, Juan asked Sam to tag along when high quantities of drugs were sold and then ordered him to go when his thug friends strongarmed noncompliant drug distributors. Juan used intimidation to get Sam directly involved in some serious crimes with some of his criminal friends. He ordered Sam to meet some of his friends for killing without telling him what they would do in advance. All Sam had to do was s check to make sure the person was dead. But he was so terrified when he saw who it was, he lied that the person was killed, and the person survived. Juan thought Sam was stupid and hadn't checked close enough. He was infuriated when he found out. But it angered him even more than his friends hadn't followed up either. They knew better. They would have to clean up their mess eventually. It also meant that Sam was increasingly losing the little value he had to Juan.

For Sam, Juan's use of violence to enforce his rules was downright terrifying. He had a lot of power, and some of his friends were hardened criminals who wouldn't think twice about killing anyone.

One Monday, Sam reported to work and was looking at a list of service calls. When he was assigned to leave on a repair job that morning, he got delayed because he couldn't find some parts and started rummaging in the back. While there, he accidentally witnessed a chilling incident. Three of Juan's friends forcibly dragged a young man inside the shop, and to his amazement, Juan brutally beat the young man with a big metal flashlight while hollering profanities in Spanish.

He struck him so hard that the flashlight came apart, and the batteries bounced on the floor. Once the man was down, the other two men started kicking him, and he heard yelps and groans as the victim curled into a fetal position and covered his head with his arms. The young man was bleeding from the nose and one of his ears and had a nasty cut above his left eye. He was obviously in excruciating pain. Once the kicking stopped, he slowly struggled to his feet and stumbled into the wall, trying to keep his balance. He looked terrified and was whimpering that he was sorry, as Juan's two thugs took him outside and pushed him into the back of a car, and then sped away. At that moment, Sam looked up and noticed that Juan was staring at him with an angry expression.

"How come you're still here? You're supposed to be out on the job! You're already late!" Juan snapped.

Sam gathered himself and answered, "Of course not. I had to find the right couplings for some of the tubing I needed for the job on the fifth street, and it was hard to find the right sizes."

"You didn't see nothin', right?" Juan growled.

Sam was momentarily paralyzed with a blank stare and open mouth. Juan repeated, "Right?!"

"Right!"

"Get the fuck outta here now!" Juan shouted as he threw the remaining pieces of the flashlight against the wall.

Sam immediately left the shop but could feel Juan's eyes burning a hole into his back as he got into the company van and started driving towards his appointment. What he witnessed kept racing through his head like a video replay. He was so upset that he couldn't remember the trip there when he arrived at the site. He had a hard time concentrating while he was doing the repair job too. His mind kept shifting to the two men who strongarmed the young male into Juan's shop. They all were wearing khakis and T-shirts. There were tattoos, but he couldn't remember what they were. They were words and symbols.

Everything had happened so fast and was so cruel he was still in panic mode. He tried to remember their faces just in case he encountered them in the future, but he couldn't remember much. He feared what they may have done with the victim after they left the shop and realized that he might already be in deep trouble, and there didn't seem to be a way out.

Sam was now contemplating gathering his belongings and running away. But he knew that Juan wouldn't stand for it. He'd probably send his posse after him and beat or maybe even kill him. Panic was now taking over him.

While driving back to the shop, Sam was apprehensive about what Juan was going to do with him since he had witnessed the beating. When he arrived, he wanted to get in and out of the shop as quickly as possible. When he entered the shop through the bay area, he saw Juan on the phone in the office. Sam brought his paperwork and placed it in Juan's in-basket. Juan motioned him to sit down, finished the call, and hung up. He appeared calmer.

"How did the job go?" he asked.

"It went fine. The repairs were perfect," Sam answered.

"Good. I wanna talk to you about this morning. That guy you saw stole some money from me. I had to teach him a lesson. Nobody crosses me."

"I get it," Sam replied.

"Do you? Just remember, what happens in this shop stays here, and no betrayal goes unpunished! Understood?" Juan demanded as he slammed his fist on his desk.

"Loud and clear," Sam trembled.

Juan studied Sam silently for a few minutes and then looked over the paperwork for the service call. "I might have some more special projects for you in the future, and I don't take no for an answer. Got it?"

"Yes, sir," Sam nodded.

Juan motioned him to leave, so he got up and left the office immediately.

After leaving work, Sam decided to return to Becky's home to have a few beers while thinking about what might happen next on his job. When he entered through the front door, he couldn't stop thinking about what had gone down that day. Becky had left a note that she would be home late from work and not to stay up. He removed a Bud Light beer from the His hand lifted the beer to his lips for a sip but were shaking so much he put it back on the coffee table. He then moved to the den and turned on the widescreen TV with the remote control. He scrolled through the channels until he got to a music channel and settled back onto the sofa. He kept wondering about how much Becky knew about Juan.

Sam's mind was racing. He knew Juan was a big-time operator, and he was becoming a part of it. Selling drugs at such a high level smelled of the Cartel, and he knew Juan would order him to do things much more damning, and it would tie him to a life worse than death. It would make it impossible for him to return to the stress-free life he once had unless he could somehow disappear.

Chapter 12

Jane and I had decided to meet at my house to relax, and she brought Bailey. He acted like he was glad to see me, and soon after they arrived, Bailey settled onto a pillow I had put on the living room floor. Jane agreed to help me navigate Google to find out more about me. But when we sat down on the sofa, I turned on the TV, and rather than doing research, we kept watching TV. Bailey quickly joined us and settled on Jane's lap. We scanned the cable TV channels and settled on watching an episode of "Outlander." Neither of us was watching it, though, and the silence was deafening. Both of us were preoccupied, thinking about what was discussed during our visit to the shelter.

I tried to piece together what Jane had told me about the history of our relationship. It sounded like it was severe, but my actions and her accident had derailed it. It was unfortunate that I hadn't waited to let her get her memory back in her own time when she got hurt. I had pressured her because I didn't trust her. I thought she was faking it. That turned out to be the last straw on the camel's back for her.

But now, my romantic connection with her made it uncomfortable when thinking about what to do next.

Jane asked, "What are you thinking about?"

"I'm thinking about us," I answered. "I'm trying to envision what's next. And if I pressured you when you couldn't remember things, I apologize. It was wrong."

Jane didn't respond but looked away.

I exhaled loudly. My hand was resting on hers. After holding my hand for a moment, she leaned and placed her head on my shoulder.

I looked down into her eyes, and she smiled, "It'll be fine." Then she kissed me lightly on the lips. That simple kiss stirred my desire and apprehension at the same time. I couldn't remember enough about all the drama surrounding the breakups and felt vulnerable. But I kissed her again. Only this time, it was long and passionate.

"I never stopped loving you, Ken," Jane whispered.

"Well, I can't imagine how I could have felt any different than I do now," I answered.

"And what is that?".

"It's a special feeling, but I can't say the words yet."

Jane closed her eyes as her body seemed to melt into mine. She kissed me again but with more intensity. I gently moved my hand to her chin and lifted her face towards mine so she could look into my eyes, and whispered, "I don't know if I can hold back from what I am thinking about doing to you right now."

Her blue-green irises narrowed, as her pupils dilated. My mind was seeing road signs, "Proceed with caution," but my strong urges were saying, "step on the gas!"

"So, what are you waiting for?" She asked with a mischievous grin.

I must have had a momentary expression of panic because Jane quickly added, "We can slow things down if you want. It's okay."

But the passion was sidelining my brain, and after a few more moments, I shook my head and answered, "It feels right. It feels... perfect."

She stood up and extended her hand, and I held on as she pulled me up from the sofa. We slowly made our way to the bedroom as we continued to kiss and touch each other. We were cautious at first after laying on the bed, but it quickly turned into a night of pure lust. Heavy breathing and the sounds of the headboard bouncing off the wall echoed outside the room. After the sounds of orgasmic moans, there was a long period of quiet. It brought some strong feelings of Deja vu with it.

Jane went to sleep quickly. She seemed relieved, and I felt happy, but I knew things would not be entirely right until I regained full memory and knew everything about our past. Then, and only then, could I feel that our reconciliation was emotionally safe. I felt happy and worried at the same time.

I was also wondering if things were moving too fast. Either way, things were a lot more complicated now.

"Maybe I'm overthinking this," I thought.

Bailey jumped onto the bed and pushed his head under my hand just before I fell into a deep comfortable sleep.

Jane stayed the rest of the night. She seemed content, and I felt more secure than I had at any other time since that horrible night in the mountains.

The following day, I awoke gradually with the lure of an aroma of fresh coffee, and when I opened my eyes, I smiled as the smell of bacon and eggs grabbed my attention. I lifted myself from the bed and staggered towards the kitchen. My nose was following the aroma as if it were pulling me in that direction. My shorts and T-shirt were twisted, and my hair was sticking out in all directions. The toaster popped, causing me to jerk with a start. Bailey started barking and running around in circles. I patted him on the head and looked up at Jane.

Jane was standing over a skillet with a spatula and turned her head in my direction. She started laughing as her eyes looked up and down my body.

"Look at you. Aren't you a sight?" Jane laughed.

At that moment, I was hypnotized by her shapely figure partially obscured by one of my button-down shirts, and she knew how to wear it to display her physical assets.

I smiled and said, "I'm sure that you look a hundred times better in that shirt than I do."

Jane looked pleased with the compliment.

She tilted her head and continued to scan my body, "Well, I guess I've seen you at your worst and still wanna jump your bones. But not before we eat!" she laughed.

I then gave a mischievous smile.

"Do you have anything on under that shirt?"

She turned away, "That's for me to know and for you to find out."

I turned her around and kissed her lips gently as she held the spatula off to the side. We hugged for a full minute, and I could feel the intense positive energy flowing between us.

I sat down at the table, and Jane handed me a hot cup of coffee with cream and sugar. She purposely brushed her body against mine as she walked back to the stove. It felt good and very familiar. I thought about it and closed my eyes.

"Were we always like this?"

"Yes, we were like this all the time. It was easy."

"I think I remember that feeling. But did you always dress like that when you served coffee to me?"

Jane laughed and stood next to me.

"No, this is new. Do you like it?"

"Are you kidding? What's not to like?

Jane smiled and sat at the table.

"By the way, what do you think about going to my parent's house tonight?" We could visit, and it might bring back some memories," she offered.

After a thoughtful pause, I answered, "Well, that might be alright, but what did your parents think of me during the time we were having all the conflicts? If I were them, I'm not sure I would have liked that version of me."

"I admit that when they found out I had taken you back before the accident, they weren't too thrilled. When you told my parents at the hospital, they were disappointed at first. By then, they knew about the cheating. My father, especially, repeatedly reminded me about what you did. I know they were both relieved when I broke up with you again the second time, but they were only being protective."

"I can understand that." I answered.

She put her hand on my shoulder and added, "But they knew I was looking for you again, and they knew I wanted to get back with you. They have been supportive. Before they found out that you had cheated on me, they liked you a lot then too."

"That's good to know. I guess it wouldn't hurt to visit with your parents."

Jane looked concerned. "Ken, remember if it's too much for you, tell me, and we can slow things down. I don't want you to feel overwhelmed."

"I will," I answered.

Then Jane changed the subject, "Officer Taylor seems to think that finding Sam will be an important step in solving the crime against you."

"Yes, he seems to think that Sam was involved. I hope he finds him."

Jane nodded and started putting their dishes in the sink. She appeared to be happy and kept smiling at me as she cleaned the dishes.

After we took our showers, Jane put Bailey on a leash and left for her apartment.

During the rest of the day, I felt like I was on a cloud and emotionally charged. It was a fantastic experience. I cleaned the house and spent the rest of the day navigating Google but could not find any helpful information. Jane and I had agreed that I would show up at about 6:30 pm that night, so at 5:00 pm, I changed into some clean clothes. At 6:00, I was ready to go.

After locking up, I backed out of my driveway and started towards her parent's house. I was feeling optimistic and felt more self-assured. Jane had given detailed directions on how to get to her parents, remembering that I wouldn't know the location. When I finally arrived at the front of their house, nothing about the white ranch-style home or neighborhood looked familiar to me. The brown trim and the matching wood-stained door were a mirror image of several houses on that block.

I felt a little anxious as I approached her front door, but Jane opened the door before I stepped onto the porch.

"Hi, Ken. Come on in."

Mrs. Conners came to her side and smiled.

"Hello, Mrs. Connors," I said.

"How've you been, Ken?"

"I'm doing fine. But things have been quite an adventure."

"That's what I've been hearing."

When we walked into their living room, Jane's father, Jack, held a newspaper at his side in front of an easy chair. He shook my hand and then motioned for me to sit down on the sofa. Jane sat next to me and took my hand into hers. Her parents sat across from us in a love seat.

"I heard about your injuries Ken. Are you alright?" Mr. Connors asked with a concerned expression.

"I'm just trying to find my memory. My physical recovery appears to be nearly complete. Your daughter has been very helpful with filling in some of the missing pieces from my past. I wouldn't even be close to where I am now had it not been for her."

"Can you remember anything?" Mrs. Connors asked.

"Just small bits and pieces. I do not remember events or places as much as feelings, like Déjà vu experiences. The doctor said he was confident that most or all of it would come back pretty soon," I added.

"That's good," Mr. Connors acknowledged. "Jane has been through the same thing, and it was hard on everyone."

Jane nodded her head and answered, "It was frightening for me too.

The four of us visited for about an hour, talking about things we had done in the past. Jane's parents talked more about how difficult it was for them when Jane was trying to recover from the physical injuries. It had taken a while to walk normally again. But she had fully recovered, and things had gotten back to normal. They were also happy that she had gotten her apartment and was on her own. She was also doing well on her job so far.

The more we talked, the atmosphere relaxed. Jane's parent's concern for me seemed genuine. Nothing about our breakups was mentioned, and nothing was uncomfortable or awkward.

When we left and returned to my house, Jane gave me a long and passionate kiss before leaving in her car. It was a replica of the one that had been totaled in her accident. It was Sunday, so she had to work the next day, and so did I. Optimism filled the air because the last two days had been productive, and my mind had settled a great deal.

As she disappeared on the road, I wondered, "Why in the hell did I cheat on her? What the hell was wrong with me?"

When I went into my house, I started reminiscing about how Jane and I had reconnected. It was a very emotional experience, and it helped me in the aftermath of the trauma, and the sex was exceptional.

Jane texted me to let me know she had arrived at her apartment safely. She left a heart-shaped emoji, and I returned the same.

Apprehension still haunted me when I thought about what it would be like when my memory returned. I tried not to think about it.

I checked all the locks on the doors and windows of the house before I went to bed and saw a sheriff's unit slowly passing the front of the house. I watched until he disappeared.

I was exhausted. Before I fell asleep, I wrote myself a note to call a security company and have an alarm installed in my home. It was the safest thing I could do for now.

Chapter 13

Sam was glad that Becky was out of town on a business trip. There was too much pressure, and he didn't need Becky asking questions. He needed to make some decisions about Juan's increasing criminal demands. Sam had realized that Juan had set him up, and at this moment, he had no idea what he was going to do, but he knew it had to happen soon. Sam hadn't only sold a lot of drugs but had skimmed some of it for himself. It hadn't been much, but he figured that Juan would kill him if he found out.

Leaving New Mexico and starting over might work, but he would miss Becky and no telling what she would do to get even. She had told him once that she had always gotten even when someone crossed her. The tragic reality was that leaving her was the least dangerous of all his options.

Sam knew that Juan wouldn't let it go if he tried to disappear. His posse might come after him and either beat or kill him. No matter what, something had to give. He might end up as a "mule" for Juan's drug trafficking. Like it or not, he was a part of Juan's gang of thugs. The stakes were getting higher and higher, and it was only going to get worse. For now, he had to appear strong and self-confident in front of Juan because Juan was already thinking he was weak and becoming a liability. He had seen enough to know that Juan wouldn't hesitate to kill him if he thought Sam was in the way.

Sam called in sick that day so he could clear his mind. Juan seemed suspicious but was busy with a customer on the other line and said he would see Sam the following day. Before ending the conversation, he told Sam that he had something important to do, and it had to be done the next day. It was an apparent demand, and Sam was sure that Juan would tell him to do something very illegal. Sam assured Juan that he would do whatever he was asked. He knew he had to say that, but going down that road was looking more and more like a suicide mission. Juan's call raised his anxiety even more and ruined the rest of his day. He felt like his life was in danger and couldn't stop thinking about what Juan might do next.

Sam couldn't sleep that night and used the time to run possible scenarios through his mind on ways to escape his dilemma. Unfortunately, his former friend, Ken, was cool-headed and had been a helpful friend in the past when Sam had gotten himself into trouble, but he was no longer available.

Sam arrived at his job at 7:25 am the next day. Juan usually met with him and another worker, Jose Gonzales, at 7:30 to ensure that the day's job assignments were laid out. Jose was nowhere to be found. Juan said that he had already left for an all-day job in Los Lunas, south of Albuquerque.

Juan gave Sam a cup of coffee and then motioned for him to sit at the desk in his small office. Sam sat quietly, waiting for Juan to give him whatever orders he had. Juan leaned back in his chair and folded his arms, looking Sam squarely in the eyes.

"I have a job for you to do."

"Okay, what's up?"

"I need for you to go with one of my boys to Santa Fe and make a delivery."

"Okay, so what are we delivering?"

"All you need to know is that it's precious cargo mixed with plumbing supplies. The less you know, the better, so don't ask questions. Just follow orders."

Sam thought for a moment and then nodded, "Who are we making the delivery to?"

"You're already asking questions pendejo!" he grumbled. "Don't worry about it! My friend Hector will do all the talking and make the transaction. You just be there in case you're needed! Nothing more and nothing less! If you can fuck up doing nothing, there is no hope for you!"

Sam frowned. "No disrespect, but if this doesn't have anything to do with plumbing, I would rather not go. I still have repairs to do with an appointment for this afternoon."

Juan walked up and stabbed Sam in the chest twice with his index finger causing him to take two steps back. Their noses were almost touching.

"What the fuck Sam? Do you really think this is a negotiation? You're going and that's it! You're starting to piss me off and you don't wanna ever do that!"

Sam didn't back down. "I'm sorry, but all I want to do from now on, is plumbing. If I can't, I'll quit this job!"

Juan smirked and quickly kicked Sam in the crotch. Then he punched him in the solar plexus, causing him to crumble to the floor, groaning as he gasped for air.

Now Juan was gritting his teeth. "You just don't get it, do you? I own you now, you dumb fuck! You need me, and I don't need you! You're lucky to have Becky, or you'd be six feet under already!" If you wanna stay alive, you'd better get in line! What's it gonna be?"

Sam was still clutching his midsection and gasping for air. He was pale and dizzy. He was worried that Juan might kill him at this moment. With his heart pounding and panic growing, he looked at Juan and put his hand up in resignation.

"Well, I guess I am going to Santa Fe after all."

"Damned right you are!" Juan snapped. "From now on, I'm gonna be watching you real close and so are my guys. Don't ever say no to me again when I tell you to do something! You've used up eight of your nine lives! Got it?"

"Yes, sir! What time do we leave?" Sam gasped.

"About three. Hector will come and get you."

Sam called Becky at noon and told her he might be late because he had to go to Santa Fe at 3:30 in the afternoon and didn't know how long the delivery would take. She asked him to call her when he was on his way back, and he agreed.

"But would he still be alive by then?" he wondered.

At 3:00 pm, Hector Dominguez tapped him on the shoulder and motioned him to follow. He was only about 5'6" and maybe weighed 130-135 pounds. But he was very rugged and covered with tattoos. He was driving a white Dodge Van without the company placard from the shop. It had several boxes in the back. After introducing them, Juan ordered Sam to do whatever Hector told him.

"It's just like I told you, Sam. Don't fuck it up! Got it?"

"Yes, I understand."

Hector was quiet during most of the drive on Highway 14 to Santa Fe. He told Sam to play it cool. He said that there would be two persons receiving the delivery. He brought Sam, so they were even in numbers.

Sam asked, "Why is that important?"

"It's just smart. It keeps things equal, and nobody gets any ideas. Nothing's going to happen, though," Hector laughed. "Don't worry, if anyone gives us a problem, I brought a friend who'll do all the talking for us." He reached down under his seat and partly slid out a 9mm so Sam could see it, and then slid it back.

Now Sam was terrified. He felt trapped. What if something went wrong? Getting killed wasn't the worst thing that could happen. He might end up in prison, and he knew he wouldn't be able to handle it. Just as he was thinking about prison, he caught a glimpse of the New Mexico State Penitentiary off to his left as they passed it. The old prison had one of the worst riots in the history of the U.S. Many inmates were tortured to death. There were new structures, but the past was still there.

Sam felt like he had no friends left in Albuquerque and just wanted to go for good. But he was sure that it wouldn't be easy to pull off. At the very least, Juan had too much on him, and his life seemed like it was over.

Hector and Sam arrived and parked in a secluded lot near an old outlet center just south of Santa Fe. Just across from them were two males who got out of their 2017 black Lincoln Continental with dark tinted windows simultaneously. They stood next to each other, looking at us. One was a stocky Hispanic man wearing jeans and a T-shirt. Sam could see a bulge under his T-shirt, and he was sure it was a weapon. The other male was an African American who was much taller, wearing a black pullover sweatshirt with LA Lakers emblazoned on the front. He was wearing a black baseball cap with a Laker's logo on the front and black jeans. Neither of the two men looked friendly. It was a serious meeting with only a few spoken words. But everything went smoothly, and the exchange was courteous. No names were mentioned.

Sam kept his mouth shut as he helped remove some of the boxes from the van. He and Hector stepped back as the two men checked the contents, inspected it, and smiled at each other. The Hispanic male nodded his head at Hector as the African American male showed Hector the contents of a briefcase before handing it to him. Sam could see a 9mm tucked in his belt behind his back. Hector was satisfied with the contents and nodded while he was slipping it inside his shirt. The Hispanic male took a small package from one of the boxes into his vehicle and stayed for about 10 minutes. Finally, he returned and waved at them with a huge smile. He was high. "Good shit, man!" he groaned and nodded at the African American male, who shook hands with Hector. He then glanced at Sam with a stern look, and Sam looked away. They loaded up all the boxes into the sedan and left immediately. Sam and Hector watched as they disappeared.

"Whatever it was, there was illegal stuff in those big boxes," Sam thought.

Hector laughed as they returned to the van. "There were only two boxes that counted," he laughed while starting the engine. When Sam didn't laugh, Hector put his hand on his shoulder,

"I like you, man, but you gotta loosen up. I got your back, man. And you gotta learn to keep your mouth shut around Juan. You talk back to him, and you won't stay above ground very long! Got it!"

Sam was surprised that Hector was trying to be helpful.

"Thanks, man. I'll keep my mouth shut from now on."

"Good!"

As they drove back, Sam called Becky and told her he was heading back to Albuquerque. He was relieved for now but had made up his mind to get out of New Mexico. He realized that there was nothing good about his situation and the reality was that there were more bad outcomes than good ones if he stayed as Juan's employee. It meant he would be in real danger, so he was going to have to hide.

When Hector and Sam returned to the shop, he and Hector visited Juan, who was waiting for them. Hector reported that it all went down without a hitch. He then handed the briefcase to Juan. When Juan inspected the cash inside, he nodded approvingly, slammed it shut, and pointed at Sam.

"How did this fuck do?"

"He didn't do nothin' but take up space, but he didn't fuck it up either," Hector laughed.

Juan snapped the fasteners on the briefcase and immediately headed towards the door without looking back.

"Okay, you guys get the fuck outta here!"

Hector gave a victory sign towards Sam as he left. Juan was satisfied.

Sam was relieved that the activity was over but was also distraught.

He had no friends to turn to and couldn't even talk to his girlfriend about it. When he got into his car, he took a deep breath. His life was out of control. When he started the engine and left the parking lot, he watched Hector and Juan standing next to their cars and talking about something. He was sure they were talking about him.

"Were they planning ways to eliminate him?' he wondered. "If not, what was Juan going to ask him to do next?" For the first time in his life, Sam felt like his days were numbered, like an animal waiting for slaughter.

When Sam returned home, Becky was having some wine and watching TV. When he walked towards her, she motioned him to stop.

"Do you want some wine?"

Sam hesitated and then nodded as she poured him a glass. When they went into the spacious living room Becky sat on the couch and patted the cushion next to her signaling him to sit beside her. Sam complied and kissed her on the lips before the cushions sank beneath him.

"How was work today?" she asked.

"I'd prefer not to talk about it.".

"Is Juan giving you a hard time? Because if he is, I can talk to him and tell him to lay off of you."

She could feel Sam's body stiffen as he looked away. She could tell something terrible had happened.

"Okay, tell me what happened!" She demanded.

"It's fine. There's nothing you can do, and if you say anything, it will just make things worse. I have to solve this problem for myself. Don't worry. I'll have it solved by the end of the day tomorrow. Everything will be fine."

Becky didn't believe him but decided to let it go.

"I have a party at work next Friday night. We're celebrating the Bank's 20th year in Albuquerque. Would you like to come as my date?" she smiled seductively.

"Yes," Sam responded. But his mind was far away, and Becky knew it.

"Sam, tell me what the hell is going on! Something is bothering you."

"It'll be okay, Becky. There's just a lot of pressure to learn and get my plumber's license, and Juan can be a prick sometimes. Just let me handle it."

Becky decided not to push it any further. There was too much silence and tension in the room after that, so she told Sam she wanted to go to bed. He kissed her before she left the room and said that he would come to bed later. But he didn't. He stayed up watching TV all night but hadn't seen anything that was on the screen. His mind was on something else far more troubling.

Chapter 14

As planned, I contacted ATD security to install cameras in the front, sides, and back of my house, including the entrances and windows. It was Saturday morning when they showed up, and I had plenty of time to stay for their tutorial on the cameras during their installation.

When ADT installed the system, I felt relieved. I went outside and tested them to see if they picked up my movement. The cameras worked better than I expected and recorded all of my activity. I was satisfied with the locations because I could see them on every side of the house.

I face-timed Jane on my iPhone and told her that the security system was finished. I let her see the cameras as I walked around the house, and she was relieved. After all, there was plenty of evidence that I should take precautions, especially if the perpetrators learned where I lived. And by now, they probably had.

In the very beginning, the media had broadcasted that a person had been found wandering down from the mountains and was alive. So, if anyone tried to kill me, they almost certainly knew it was unsuccessful. Anyone with common sense could find out where I lived easily using Google. But then my twin brother was dead. My twin brother seemed to be the target, but I was probably a loose end. No matter what, a security system would make things safer while I was at home and record anything unusual when I was gone.

For Jane, Kelly was still a mystery, and she wondered why he never came up during our past relationship. The mystery became clearer when Jim called me this morning. He said that Kelly had records showing he had been in foster homes his entire childhood. Kelly had also had a couple of stints in detention for stealing a car and selling meth. As an adult, he spent time in treatment for heroin addiction.

Most importantly, there was no record that Kelly ever lived at the same address as me. Jim had located his first foster parents, and they told him that Kelly had been dropped off at a hospital in El Paso by an unknown person when he was still a baby. Records showed that Ken's parents initiated the foster care placement. I hoped to find out more about how Kelly had left the Garrity family and ended up in foster care, but that was all the information available. The more Jim learned about Kelly's past, the more pity I felt for him, and I wondered why my parents had taken such drastic steps.

I had tried to get the information over the phone, but of course, the school wouldn't share the information without my ID number. I decided to pay a visit to CNM the following week to get my ID renewed and see my transcripts. The process went quickly, and they restored everything. I knew I could eventually learn more about my past by locating former instructors. But that would be for later.

Jane called and asked if I would like to go with her to the Flea Market the following day. I agreed and thought it might be an excellent way to relax and take a break from all the chaos. She also asked if she could come to my house to stay the night. I was happy to oblige but worried about our safety at the flea market and my home.

When Jane showed up, she had a bucket of Kentucky Fried Chicken, green beans, biscuits, mashed potatoes, and diet coke. We stacked our plates and went into the living room where we watched an old episode of "Castle." Neither of us was paying much attention, though. Jane had already seen it and kept telling me what was going to happen. Most of our attention was on the food. It was delicious.

Jane asked me if I would rather spend the night at her apartment. Her apartment was closer to the flea market, and since she hadn't been spending as much time there, she thought it would be nice. I thought so too. Besides, it was probably safer.

We arrived at Jane's apartment at 7:30 pm. When we went inside, I immediately recognized the smell of lilacs. I also noticed how organized and clean the apartment was. I laughed as I looked around.

"Wow, I feel like a slob. Your apartment is way cleaner than mine."

"You've never been the cleanest housekeeper," she teased.

"Well, I guess I can learn something from you."

That night we spent most of our time comparing notes about what we had learned. We agreed that I wasn't very safe. I tried to contact Jim, but he wasn't answering. I decided to try the following day again.

I pulled out my smartphone and went to my ADT security application and pulled up the cameras. I looked at the recording clips, and the only movement recorded was branches swaying back and forth on the trees. I put it back into my pocket and looked up. Jane was standing in front of me with inquiringly.

"Nothing is going on at my house," I reassured.

"That's great news," she answered.

That night, our passion was again at a fever pitch. When we woke up the following day, I kissed her tenderly on the lips and gave her a proud look.

"What? No breakfast?"

"Sure, but let's clean up first."

After we both showered and got dressed, Jane made some scrambled eggs, bacon, and toast, with some coffee. While we were eating, she asked, "Have you checked your security app yet since we got up?"

"Not yet. I'll check it when after we finish eating."

"You have your phone right there. Let's check now."

I pulled my smartphone from my pocket and scrolled through his apps until I came to the ATD Pulse application. I entered my password and kept eating while I waited for the cameras to came up. When I touched the icon for video clips, only a few clips came up, but one immediately caught my attention. I studied the movement logged at 11:58 pm. Headlights entered my driveway and stopped. When the driver turned off the lights, I could see a silvery silhouette of a car. I frantically waved at Jane to come and see it as I stopped the recording. With Jane standing at my side, I restarted the recording, and we watched two shadowy male figures leave the vehicle. The two men then walked cautiously towards the house as if they were trying to be as quiet as possible. They peered through each of the windows at the front of the house, but the clip ended abruptly. In the following clip, they were coming around from the back of the house. I was alarmed because the cameras on the sides of the house hadn't picked up any motion. One of the two men had a small flashlight, using it to peer into the slight openings through the window blinds. He flashed it on the ADT sign in the front yard, and he looked up towards the cameras and said something to the other man as he pointed at the one focused on them. I wasn't able to see his face.

The two men immediately went around the building and disappeared. Again, the recording ended. When I viewed the following clip, the two men started staring at the cameras, and I noticed they had covered their faces with ski masks. Both men abruptly turned the flashlight off and quickly backed away from the camera. The last clip showed them getting into the car and slamming the doors before backing out of the driveway with the headlights off. The vehicle gradually backed into the street. The clip ended soon after they started driving east.

"I doubted that it could have been two individuals planning a burglary. I shivered when I thought about the chances of two men coming to my house to finish the job on me. Had I been there, I would have been unprepared for it.

If I wasn't sure that it was someone connected to my mountain incident, Jane was. She immediately pleaded for me to call Jim. I took her advice, but there was no answer, so I left a message: "Hey Jim, this is Ken. Give me a call. Two guys were at my house last night trying to look through the windows while I was at Jane's apartment. They looked like they were up to no good, and I wonder if they're connected to my attack. Call me on my cell. It's recorded on my security cameras."

Jane and I reviewed the recording several times over the next thirty minutes. It was very dark, so it was hard to get any details that would have helped identify the shadowy figures. We agreed that I needed to install some security lights, but I didn't want to go home for now. Since Jim hadn't returned our calls, we decided to go into Albuquerque for the day while we waited for the call.

Late that morning, we left in Jane's car and arrived at the State Fairgrounds, where the flea market was crowded with people roaming around looking at things to buy. While we were walking around, we held hands and looked at different decorations for her apartment and my house. But my mind was on the recordings, and I found myself looking around constantly, worried that I might get ambushed. In the end, there were no incidents, and we couldn't decide on anything to buy. Jane admitted that she couldn't stop thinking about the camera recordings from the night before either, so it was hard to concentrate on anything else.

As we were walking to Jane's car my phone started ringing. When I answered, I heard Jim's concerned voice on the other end.

"What's going on at your house Ken? Sorry, but I dropped my phone on the street yesterday, and it's been acting up."

"Jim, I have cameras on my house now. I checked my recordings from last night when I got up this morning at Jane's apartment. Some guys were on my property sneaking around and looking into my house around midnight. They had flashlights. I think that when they noticed the cameras, they freaked out and left. We're afraid that they might be some guys who had something to do with my abduction."

"I think you are wise to draw those conclusions. I believe ATD recordings can be saved, so you should do that."

"I'm not sure how to do it, but I will figure it out."

"How about you meet me at your house, and we'll take a look? Then I can show you how to save your recordings."

"Thanks. What time?"

"I'm heading there now."

"See you in a few."

Jane then drove us back to her apartment, and we got into my car.

From there, I drove us to my house. Jim was already there, standing outside his police unit.

Jim, Jane and I walked around the house a couple of times but saw nothing very helpful. Jim reviewed the security clips and was obviously concerned, as he nodded at me. He demonstrated the procedure for saving the clips one-by-one and then sent them to himself through a text message.

"It is so dark, it's hard to identify them on the clips, and it didn't pick up all of their movement either. But they are definitely male. It's better than nothing. Maybe I can have someone with better technical skills take a look at it in the lab. Maybe it can be enhanced."

"Have you gotten a dog?" Jim asked.

"No, I really haven't found one that I want. But getting an intimidating dog might be a good idea."

"It would be nice if you could stay at Jane's apartment for a while."

"That's not a problem for me," Jane answered as she nodded towards me.

I shook my head and said, "I'd rather stay at my house. I just can't run scared all the time. I think I need to be here."

Officer Taylor made a face showing surprise and frustration. "I think you should reconsider."

"I don't think so. I don't want anyone dictating my life."

"But it might be the cause of the end of your life," Jane insisted.

"I'll be careful, and I'll let you know of the slightest problem."

Jane shook her head and looked at the ground.

Officer Taylor interrupted, "I'm going to see if I can get the Valencia County Sheriff's Department involved with this case. I've already had a friend of mine who works for Valencia County making extra rounds in your neighborhood. I'll ask him if he can get this area patrolled every night for a while."

He then added, "But the safest thing for you, Ken, is to stay at Jane's apartment, let the Sheriff patrol at night, and make it appear that you're home with the lights and TV on. Maybe they'll make a move while you're safely away."

I shook my head again and repeated that I wanted to be at home despite Jane's disapproval.

"I think I saw a patrol car a few nights ago," I recalled. "I promise I'll let you know if I see anything else that's creepy. In the meantime,

I'm going to get some outdoor lights so I can see better. It's too dark here at night."

"That's a good idea. I'll give you a contact person from Valencia County as soon as I can," Jim responded. He shook his head and then reminded me to call if anything unusual happened.

"Get that dog as soon as you can, Ken!"

"I will. I promise I will."

"Remember, if the persons you saw were involved in your incident and have any brains at all, they know you're still alive. By now, they probably know it was because of mistaken identity, but they also know that your memory will eventually return. I'm sure they don't think it's in their best interests to let you run around if you might be able to identify them."

"I understand," I replied.

Jane looked at me and pleaded, "Please stay at my apartment for a while. It might be safer."

I hugged her tightly and replied, "No, that could put you in danger. I won't do that."

Jane was worried but nodded.

"Just remember, you can come over any time and stay. I have a security system too," urged. "And we have our security at the complex."

"I feel better knowing that," I said.

After Jim left, Jane and I looked for a shelter dog from Albuquerque's Animal Humane Society. I had decided I wanted a big enough dog to afford me some protection and have an intimidating bark, but not so big that he would be hard to handle or easily jump my fence in the backyard. I felt excited about having a dog for security but also companionship. That would make me feel safer, and the barking might discourage intruders. Jane thought it was a good idea too.

It turned out that no dogs fitted my needs at the Animal Humane, so we decided to be patient and wait until I found exactly what I wanted. We were feeling discouraged anyway. I took Jane home and then returned to my house.

Later that evening, Jane was worried about me, but she felt Jim and I had done everything we could to make things as safe as possible since I was stubborn about staying there. She urged me to call her if I saw anything suspicious.

At 8:00 that night, I sat and watched an NCIS New Orleans episode but fell asleep on the couch soon after it started. About an hour later, I woke up with a start when I heard a noise outside. My heart was pounding in my chest, and I wondered if I had made a mistake staying there. After glancing at the clock, I mentally noted that it was only 9:15 pm. I got up quickly and crept into the kitchen, grabbing the bat I had next to the refrigerator. I turned off the TV and lamp next to the couch to see outside the house without being easily seen. My hands were shaking as I carefully peeked through the picture window blinds next to the front door. I sighed with relief when I saw a badge reflecting off the light from the porch as a Valencia County Sheriff's Deputy approached the front door from his Unit, which was parked in my driveway. He was a large Hispanic man in his late twenties or early thirties and was well over six feet with an athletic frame covered with a well-pressed tan uniform. He was armed with a Glock with clips on the other side of his belt. His black hair was cropped short on the sides, and I noticed that he had huge hands as he reached for the doorbell. When he rang the doorbell, and I answered immediately.

"Hi, I'm Officer Jerry Montoya, and I'm just doing a welfare check. Everything okay?"

His voice was deep and commanding, with a slight Spanish accent.

"Yes, officer, I was watching TV and fell asleep. I heard your car door shut. It scared the crap out of me. I guess I'm kind of jumpy."

Officer Montoya smiled and asked if he could have a look around, and I agreed. He took a quick walk around the house, surveying the property with his flashlight. He returned and handed me a business card with his cell phone number.

"I know Jim Taylor really well. He asked me to watch out for you. If you see anything suspicious, you can call me directly at the number on that card."

"Thanks, officer, that makes me feel better, I replied. "I just got a new security system with cameras and am still learning to use them. I just realized I could have checked who was outside with my phone. I'll do that from now on."

"I noticed the cameras," the officer acknowledged. "Don't forget, you can download any of the recordings or take still shots if any of them catches suspicious activity."

"Yes, when they installed the cameras, they explained everything, and I have already downloaded some video with Jim's help."

I watched Officer Montoya walk to his Unit and slowly back his Unit out onto the road. As he disappeared, I put the card in my wallet and took a deep breath.

I glanced at the clock again, and it was 9:50 pm. The stress and lateness caused fatigue to set in. I stretched my arms upward, shook my body, and then yawned. I sent Jane a good night text and reassured her that I had gotten a visit from Officer Montoya, who checked the immediate area. All was fine. She texted back with a heart emoji.

I went to bed and fell into a deep sleep. If there were any dreams that night, I couldn't remember them. Had anyone been looking through my windows, I would have never noticed. But I was refreshed when my alarm clock sounded. After showering and getting dressed, I checked the security recordings and was relieved to find nothing unusual. I locked the doors before getting into my car and heading to the shelter.

When I arrived at the shelter at 7:00 am, breakfast was ready, and as usual, I helped on the serving line. Watching all of the homeless persons as they got their trays made me remember how I had gotten to know many of them on a personal level. Every one of them had a unique story. The majority had some mental illness, and many were either in danger of getting hurt or hurting others. It was a shame to think about how the wealthiest country in the world seemed to have abandoned the mentally ill. Poorly run mental institutions had been shut down in the latter part of the 20th Century, replacing them with nothing better. In the short time I had been there, I had seen some of them leave for a couple of weeks and come back to the shelter in serious physical condition. They were fortunate that Reverend Myers was in their lives. He was very resourceful in getting them help, and he treated them all with the utmost respect.

Many of the homeless men and women had drug and alcohol problems too. Health consequences from addiction had burdened many of them, and many were suffering from hepatitis C, HIV, and cirrhosis of the liver.

It was a unique learning experience because of my memory loss. My condition had given me the rare opportunity of looking at myself from an outsider's point of view. It also helped me embrace a unique idea of humanity. From watching this part of it, I had come to believe that all humans were blessed with a virtuous side and, at the same time, cursed with an evil nature. They were often conflicted with each other. It seemed that one or the other tipped that scale and determined if the person was good or bad. I was still confident that the good was dominant in most people. Unfortunately, the stories I heard made me astutely aware that evil always seems close by. It appeared that corruption often interrupts the good in us, but most of us overcome it. I often wondered which of the two dominated the real me. I still didn't know if the attempt on my life was because of something I witnessed or knew or if I had been involved in a criminal enterprise and maybe crossed one or more of my partners in crime. I figured that if I was good at being bad, no one outside that circle would know about it, except the old me.

I had also learned that people like Reverend Myers were pretty rare. His contributions to humanity were pure. He had made me understand that he believed that spreading goodwill was best when there was no expectation for recognition from others. Nothing he did seemed to be out of obligation either. Kindness was as natural as breathing for him. He never looked for applause. He was the perfect person for what he was doing and was an excellent example for everyone around him. I felt lucky to know him.

Chapter 15

Sam was driving towards Juan's Plumbing for another day of stress and misery. But as he got close to the freeway exit, he had a severe panic attack when he noticed a single word texted from Hector. "Run!"

Sam fumbled with his phone as he returned the text, "Why?" There was no answer.

After waiting for a few minutes, he decided he couldn't take it anymore. For some strange reason, Hector had taken a liking to him and was looking out for him. His text meant that Sam was in imminent danger.

Sam suddenly realized his life was on the line and worth more than his relationship with Becky. He needed to make a decision right now. Sam found himself passing his exit and driving straight through Albuquerque, continuing through the Sandia mountains. After some desperate thinking, he thought about his cousin Chris who lived in Amarillo. He decided to keep going until he reached his cousin's apartment and hoped he could hide there.

Since Sam hadn't shown up for work, Juan called three times throughout the day. The last time he called, he left a message for Sam telling him that he would pay with his hide for not calling in sick. But maybe he hadn't considered Sam wasn't ill.

In the meantime, Sam was getting away from what had turned into a personal hell. He stopped a few times on the way and even stayed at a rest stop for three hours to clear his head and keep from turning back.

Later in the day, Hector came to the job site. Juan was in a bad mood.

"Have you seen or heard from Sam? I've been trying to call him all day. Like I told you, he's been stealing drugs from us!"

Hector tried to hide his fear.

"No, I haven't seen him since we got back from Santa Fe."

Juan looked at Hector suspiciously, and Hector looked down at the floor.

"I'm going to ask you one more time! Have you heard from Sam?"

"No, I haven't."

"Let me see your fucking cell phone bitch!"

Hector was caught off-guard and acted like he was searching his pockets, but Juan looked like he might do a body search. He reached for his phone, and when he handed it to Juan, he was visibly shaking.

"Put in your password Cabron!"

"Why the fuck do you wanna look at my cell phone?"

"Because I want to, and you're gonna let me!"

Hector punched in his password, and Juan snatched it from his grip. He started scrolling down his Email and shook his head. Then he started scrolling Hector's text messages.

"You mother fucker! You told him to run! Where's he going?"

Hector was gasping for air. "I have no idea!"

"I'll deal with you later traidor! We're gonna find that asshole and take care of him permanently! Then I'm gonna teach you a lesson you won't forget!! We're gonna make some plans to end Sam's shit! But you're gonna be the mother fucker to do it, right in front of me."

Meanwhile, Sam was well on his way to Texas. He usually returned from work to Becky's home at around 5:30 pm or called her when he would be late.

Becky was surprised when she came home from work at six and Sam wasn't there. She sat on her living room sofa with a glass of wine, waiting for him so that she could find out what was going on with Juan, and figured it would be an excellent opportunity to calm him down. His recent behavior had been disturbing, and she needed to get to the bottom of it. Sam had been evasive when she had pressured him to tell her about his problem with Juan, but it seemed to make him more uncomfortable.

It was now 8:00 pm, and Sam was nowhere to be found. He hadn't called or texted her. When she dialed his number, it went straight to the voicemail, and he wasn't answering her text messages. Her anger was growing, but she was also getting worried.

Becky contacted Juan at 8:30 pm to see if Sam was working late. When she asked him about it, the line went quiet for a few moments. She thought they had been disconnected. "Hello?"

"Ah… no…. he never showed up for work. I thought he was sick. He's not with you?"

"What the…?" Becky stopped. "Okay, Juan. If you hear from him, let me know, and please tell him to call me."

"I will, and you call me if he contacts you or comes home, okay?"
"I will… Thanks, Juan."

After she hung up, Sam's absence filled her with worry, suspicion, and anger.

"Just wait until he comes home!" she thought. "He'd better have a good explanation!"

In the meantime, Sam had just passed Bushland, heading east on I-40, just outside of Amarillo. He had finally devised a plan. His cousin, Chris Glew, worked for the Amarillo Gas Company as a Distribution Lineman apprentice. Sam felt pretty confident Chris would let him stay long enough to get back on his feet. His cousin had just gotten a divorce and had moved to a new apartment just a few months ago. He was unhappy because he had to pay child support and needed a shoulder to cry on. He trusted Sam and looked up to him. But Sam would have to make sure he didn't say anything that would spook Chris into turning him away. He decided to ask Chris to let him stay there for a while. The phone rang several times, and just when he was about to hang up, Chris saw his name on the caller ID and answered. "Hi, Sam. What's up?"

"I just broke up with my girlfriend, and I need a place to get off the radar. Do you think I could stay at your place for a while?"

After a brief pause, Chris answered, "Sure, man. I could use the company. But I can't give you a free ride. With the child support and all that, I'm just barely making it."

"I got paid just before this past weekend, and I have some money saved up. I can help out with some bills until I can get a job," Sam replied.

"Seriously? You're gonna leave Albuquerque after all these years, just like that? On top of that, I thought you were in L-O-V-E with this girl."

"Sometimes, you just have to change directions and try something completely new," Sam replied. "My life has just gotten too complicated in Albuquerque, and it doesn't feel like home anymore. I'm breaking up with my girlfriend because I need a new start, and I know she'll never leave there. I know she's gonna be pissed when I tell her I'm breaking it off so it will be good to be far away from her."

"You mean you haven't told her yet?"

"Unfortunately, no,"

"Wow! You're too much, man! What time do you think you'll get here? Do you need directions?"

"I'm right outside Amarillo. I need to get to your apartment. I have your address and Google Maps. There shouldn't be a problem. If I get lost, I'll call you."

Chris was shocked that Sam was so close to Amarillo.

"Wow, you don't waste any time, do you? I guess I'll see you in a few."

Sam had a 1998 Ford F-150 with 200,000 miles on it. But it was still in excellent running condition. He was a pretty good mechanic and did most of the major repairs, including an engine overhaul. He had even done body repairs and had it repainted sapphire blue, which made it look new.

As Sam had gotten further from Albuquerque, he felt relieved and was sure he made the right decision. Nothing was worth risking his life, except for Becky, and he would be no good for her if he was dead. It was just too dangerous for him and maybe her. If she found out about the drugs, she would probably kick him out anyway. It was a no-win scenario. He was ready to start over and use this bad experience to make better choices for the future.

In the meantime, Becky was at home angrily pacing back and forth, adding more wine to the flame. She wondered if he was out with another woman. If that was the case, he was going to have to find somewhere else to live. She wasn't the type to tolerate infidelity and couldn't conceive of a reason why any man would want to cheat on someone like her.

Finally, at 10:00 pm, she sat back on the couch with another glass of wine. She decided to contact Sam's old girlfriend, Katie. Maybe she knew something. She dialed and waited as the phone rang.

"Hello?"

"Hello, is this Katie?"

"Yeah, this is Katie. Who is this?"

"Uh... this is Becky. I'm sure you don't want to talk to me, but I don't know what else to do. Sam seems to have disappeared, and I can't get ahold of him, even on his cell phone. I'm worried about him. Have you heard from him?"

"How would I know? It sounds like little Sammy's out doing what he's best at. How does it feel?"

Becky paused and took a deep breath. "I know you think he cheats on everyone, but this is different. I think something's wrong."

"He's the Sam we all come to know and love. Goodbye! Get used to it!"

"Yes, but... hello? Hello?

Katie had hung up, and Becky was discouraged. She stayed up until midnight, hoping he would show up. But with all the alcohol in her system, Becky couldn't keep her eyes open. The empty wine glass eventually rolled down onto the carpet next to the couch as she rested her head against the back of the sofa. The next thing she knew, it was 6:00 am, time to get up, shower, and get ready for work. She hadn't even changed into her nightwear. And she had a nasty hangover that made her feel like someone had beaten her on the head.

After several cups of coffee, Becky drove to work and arrived at 8:30 am. She tried to contact Sam several times but had no luck, so she reached Juan. Juan was annoyed.

"You can do so much better than Sam. I don't know what you see in him. I haven't heard nothin from him since the day before yesterday! He's gonna pay when I get my hands on him!"

"Let's not jump to conclusions, Juan. Something might have happened to him. Don't get mad at him," she pleaded.

"We'll see," Juan muttered.

When Becky hung up the phone, she couldn't concentrate on her work. Something was wrong. She could tell that Juan was more than just disappointed with Sam and wondered what to do next. Her father, Gerald, and Juan had a close connection, so she considered talking to him about this situation, hoping he could persuade Juan to be more patient with Sam. Juan recognized the power and prestige of her father. He would probably back off if her father demanded it.

Becky called her father and explained all that had happened. Her father seemed irritated.

"You know I never really liked that prick, right?"

"I know, but I do," she whined. "Help me out."

"Okay then. I'll call Juan and tell him to leave Sam alone. But I don't trust Sam, and neither should you. He doesn't have the character to make commitments to anybody but himself. How do you know he's not out with some other chica?"

"Trust me. Sam won't do that. He knows better."

"Well, I'll see what I can do. But if he doesn't have a good reason for this, I'm done!"

Fifteen minutes later, Becky received a return call from her father.

"Damn! Juan is really pissed at Sam. He told me that Sam is 'fucking up!' He said that some of his other workers were also messing up royally, and he's had it with Sam! I don't think I would like to work for Juan."

"So, what are you going to do?" Becky asked.

"Don't worry, Juan will come around. Any idea where Sam may have gone?"

"All I know is he has been upset about something, and I couldn't get him to talk about it. I think it had to do with his job. If he got mad and left, I know that he has a cousin somewhere in Texas and parents in St. Louis. That's all that he has told me."

"Alright then. If Sam contacts you, let me know, okay?" her father requested.

"Okay, I'll let you know."

"By the way, don't forget that I told you that it was a bad idea to introduce Sam to Juan. Juan's got a business to run and is a hothead. Sam has no loyalties, and I think he's weak. You can do better. Juan isn't as smart as I thought either. They are a bad combination. Our family name is at stake, and If you get tangled up into a mess, we'll have a big scandal to deal with."

"I know, I know," Becky sighed.

Her father then said, "If we find him, I think I'll just see if I can get him another job."

Becky sighed, "I hope he's still in Albuquerque."

Chapter 16

When I arrived at the Shelter for work Reverend Myers approached me and asked if I could help his new assistant, Chuck Andrews, run the Shelter while visiting his ailing brother in Cleveland, Ohio. He said he would be gone for a couple of days. His brother was in the hospital, dying of bone cancer, and had asked for him. I was honored to help and had learned enough about the daily routines that I was comfortable taking that role. Chuck was in his late fifties and was in good shape for his age. His 6' frame and deep voice had a commanding effect on the residents, making it easier to keep order. He dressed casually and understood the homeless population because he had once been in their shoes. He had worked as a volunteer for Reverend Myers' church for two years and knew the operation front and backward.

After Reverend Myers left, I immediately found Chuck, and we worked out a system to share the workload. We had a night person named Carl Mason who ran things from 10:00 pm until 6:00 am. Carl was also from the church, and he was an outgoing little man at just 5'6" and maybe 130 pounds. But the residents liked him and didn't cause him any problems. Chuck decided to work the swing shift at 2:00 pm, and I agreed to work the morning shift starting at 6:00 am. But I expected to stay later to make a smooth transition for Chuck. We also had a volunteer that helped during the swing and graveyard shifts. Maria

Pena was in her mid-seventies and was one of the graveyard volunteers who was a big help and didn't put up with any nonsense. The residents respected her. She agreed to help while the morning meal was being served. Reverend Myers had a book with law enforcement contacts, emergency medical responders, and other backup clergy members he could call if needed.

When I left for the shelter that morning, I texted Jane, "On my way to work... I will call when I get a break. ;-)"

She texted back, "Keep your eyes open... Luv u. xxx."

When I arrived at 6:00 am, Carl met me and said that one of the volunteers had already started getting the food line ready. Benny, who had become a long-term resident, was helping the food line and in the kitchen area. When Benny saw me come in, he immediately came by to say hello. He also told me that he needed to talk to me sometime that morning, and I told him I would look for him.

Even though the workers had organized the food line, it was still a lot of work. Most of the homeless men and women would not stay very long for one reason or the other. Volunteers would place some of them in an apartment, and others would leave unannounced. Some of them, including Benny, cleaned the eating area after meals and did the dishes. Carl left the shelter once he finished the dishes and cleanup.

While I was working that day, I kept thinking about some of the stories and tragedies that caused homelessness and how that could have easily happened to me. Benny told stories about his time on street corners with cardboard signs asking for work or handouts. He acknowledged that most people were kind and compassionate but that some were very cruel and aggressive. He said he received a lot of verbal abuse that included threats and that he had had half-empty cups of soda and trash thrown at him. Another man staying at the shelter remembered when he was hospitalized after being attacked by three young male teens who broke his cheekbone and orbital bone over his left eye. They seemed to be doing it just for fun.

It made me think of my own life. While I couldn't remember my past, it was still there, buried deep in my unconscious mind, and occasionally, familiar feelings would bubble to the top.

The women shared many horror stories about escaping domestic violence in the home as a significant cause for their predicament. A few of them recounted the horror of being raped and beaten. One woman told of how a pimp had introduced her to drugs and then forced her into prostitution, including beatings and constant pressure to meet quotas.

By the end of the day, I had to reevaluate my circumstances. My situation was not nearly as dreadful as the persons I had spoken to. I had a better understanding of the bias against the homeless. Many people believe that homeless people choose their predicament. It certainly wasn't valid with this group. I had a strong urge to keep helping these individuals for the rest of my life. I fully expected that my occupation would change, but that didn't mean that I wouldn't continue volunteering. A lot of the homeless were veterans who had PTSD and were not getting the treatment they needed. Reverend Myers had done an admirable job connecting many of them with some philanthropic treatment providers, but it was not nearly enough.

Before leaving the shelter, I ensured that Chuck had all the critical information from my shift and left him with my cell phone number if there was an emergency or if he had any questions. Chuck was a very independent, take-charge personality type and was confident that all would go smoothly. He had a booming voice. But his tone was jovial and friendly, so communications were easy.

When I got into my car, I checked the security video clips around my house. Except for an occasional bird flying in front of the cameras, there was nothing unusual. I sighed with relief as I left the parking lot. Then I texted Jane.

"Hey. How are you?"

After a few moments, I received a reply, "Getting ready to leave work. I'm going to my mom's house to pick up some clothes and then back to my apartment to feed my dog and have supper. Give me a call at about sevenish?"

"Okidoki," I replied.

Traffic was heavy as I drove south on I-40 during rush hour, and I found myself getting agitated at some of the rudeness of other drivers.

They never seemed to give a second thought about the danger they created for others.

Once I arrived at his house, I checked the mail and found nothing but marketing schemes. I immediately tore them up and dropped them into the trash can outside my home.

I checked my phone messages, and the first one was from Reverend Myers. He reminded me that I could call at any time if something unusual came up at the shelter and if I needed advice. He also said that things were going about as well as possible with his sister. I smiled and decided I would call him later since he seemed a little worried. All the other messages turned out to be marketing calls, so I immediately deleted them.

Because I was tired, I chose a frozen beef enchilada dinner from my freezer and microwaved it. Once it was cooked, I sat at the table and ate it slowly while sipping on a can of Coke Zero. It was pretty good for frozen food, or I was starving.

After I finished eating and settled in, I remembered that Jane was stopping off at her mother's house, so I decided to call her to see if she might want to get together. First, I dialed her cell phone number, and it went to voicemail. Then I dialed her parent's home phone. Her mother answered, "Hello?"

"Hi, Mrs. Connors. This is Ken. How are you?"

"Hi Ken, I'm doing fine. How's your memory? Is anything coming back?"

"So far, little bits and pieces are coming back but very disorganized."

"I'm so glad to hear that. Lucky for Jane, her memory came back in just a few days. Be patient. You'll get it back eventually."

When I heard those words, I didn't hear much else. After I hung up, my heart sank because I now knew that Jane had lied to me. Everything that had seemed perfect now seemed to be a lie. What would I do now, and how much more had she left out about our relationship?

At 6:30 pm, I contacted Reverend Myers and caught him up on the day's events. He had no new information about his trip, so the conversation was pretty short. Reverend Myers was pleased and seemed relieved.

After hanging up, I looked at my smartphone and noticed it was 6:35 pm, so I decided to watch the local news. There was one report that caught my interest. It was about how the U.S. government was cracking down on Shell Companies created by U.S. businesses to help Mexican Cartels launder money. I wondered if a Cartel was somehow involved in my incident.

"What a racket," I thought.

Too many Americans liked to get high, and things wouldn't change dramatically until our society addressed it. I decided that I needed to learn more about it, so I checked some Internet stories, and it was both exciting and scary.

Then my mind returned to Jane, and I kept remembering what her mother inadvertently shared. I wanted to think that her concept of a few days wasn't what it sounded like. But I was having a hard time seeing anything beyond a lie. I couldn't stop thinking about my feelings for her and how quickly they had grown. But I was more fearful about what I couldn't remember now more than ever before. I was also much less sure about the direction I wanted to go with Jane. I decided to call her. At that moment, the phone rang and startled me. I looked at the screen of my smartphone. It was Jane. "Hi Ken, watcha doin?"

"Just watching the news. Very boring stuff."

"Hmm... I have a proposal for you," she whispered in her sexiest voice.

"And what would that be?"

"What if you came over and spent the night? You could bring your clothes and leave for work from here in the morning. And it is much closer from here. I also won't worry about you if you're here. You can always check your security cameras any time to make sure nothing bad is going on there."

I conceded that it was probably the wisest thing to do. But I couldn't stop thinking about the lie. Either way, I had to talk to her but wasn't sure what to say. I kept thinking about how foolish I would feel if we ended up breaking up after all that had happened. History suggested that it was much easier for her than for me. Suddenly, my thoughts were interrupted.

"Ken, are you there?

"I think that's a great idea," I replied.

"Okay, so when can I expect you?" She asked. I didn't answer.

"Are you okay, Ken?

"Yes...about as long as it takes for me to get there."

"Okay, then I'll see you soon."

I hung up the phone without saying goodbye. I felt mixed emotions of both anger and anxiety. After I packed a duffle bag with clothes and grooming articles, I checked to make sure all of the doors and windows were locked. Once outside, I checked to make sure the exterior of the windows and doors were secure, and no one could see inside. I had all the cameras positioned the way I wanted them.

The drive to Jane's apartment was stressful, but I was still happy that she had invited me to her apartment so we could talk about why she lied. I was also prepared to return home if things didn't go well.

When I arrived, I could hear Baily barking behind the door. Jane opened the door before I could ring the bell. She had an apprehensive look on her face but stood on her toes and kissed me softly on my lips.

"I have something I want to talk to you about," I said.

Jane had a worried expression. "Okay, let's sit," as she motioned me to the couch.

"I spoke to your mom today, and she let it slip that you regained your memory in just a few days after your automobile accident. All this time, you led me to believe that you hadn't regained your memory and that you broke up with me because I was pressuring you over it. It made me feel as selfish as you claimed it was."

Jane rested her elbows on her knees and hid her face with her hands. Then she started crying. She sat there for almost a full minute before grabbing my hand.

"I was going to tell you about it, but there never seemed to be a good time. All I can say is that when I lied to you about the amnesia, you had been pressuring me and coming on so strong that I couldn't take it, so telling you that I still had no memory bought me time to sort things out. But you just kept the pressure on. I was still in a lot of pain, so I pushed you away. I have regretted it ever since."

"So, when you told me to leave, what did you do?

"You left without saying a word. I'm sure you were angry."

"After you left, I stayed mad for a while but then started to regret it.

I shook my head. "I don't know. I need some time to sort all of this out. Is there anything else you haven't told me about?"

"No, nothing else. I'm very sorry, and I hope you will forgive me."

"I can forgive pretty easily. But it makes me wonder about how easy it is for you..."

"It wasn't easy! Don't go there!"

"I have to think about all of this. It doesn't help me get things straight in my head with no memory of my past. Let's stop talking about it."

Jane sighed deeply, looked at me pleadingly, and then agreed to stop talking about it until a later time.

Jane then abruptly asked. "Is there any new information on your case?"

"I haven't heard anything new yet. I'm going to call Jim tomorrow and see where things are. He's probably pretty busy with other cases, though."

"Do you remember anytihing about, 'Sam?" she asked.

I looked around for a few the room before answering, "Doesn't ring a bell."

"Well, Sam was a very close friend of yours for a long time, but you guys had a falling out, and he told you to leave his apartment and never contact him again. As far as I know, you didn't talk to him after that. He had a girlfriend named Katie. You, me, Sam, and Katie used to get together and party sometimes, so you knew Katie pretty well. Katie and I were friends too. As I told you, you and Sam cheated on us, and Sam got gonorrhea. Sam and Katie had to get treated, but not you. Katie said that soon after we broke up, Sam met, Becky Espinosa, and dumped Katie." She paused for a moment as she watched my reaction.

"Are you remembering anything?"

I looked at her and said. "Nothing." Then I looked to the side and closed my eyes. "Was Katie's hair blonde?"

Jane sat up straight with a smile and said, "Yes, sort of a dirty blond."

I smiled and slowly nodded. "I'm having a good feeling about Katie."

"Yes, she is a nice person. We still keep in touch. How would you like for us to visit with her and see if she can help you remember anything?" Jane was excited as she looked inquiringly into my eyes.

"That's a good idea. I think the more people that I meet that I used to know, the quicker my memory will come back."

Jane pulled her smart iPhone out and called Katie on face time. She moved to screen so both she and Ken could see who was on each end of the phone. In a few seconds, Katie answered, "Hi Jane. What's up?"

"Ken is here with me."

Katie and Ken smiled simultaneously. Katie waved and laughed, "How the hell have you been? Jane tells me you lost your memory.

That's correct. But it's good to talk with another person that I have known. How have you...?"

Jane interrupted, "Hey Katie, how would you like to meet with us to visit and talk about old times and see if we can jog Ken's memory a little?" It might help Ken remember and also give you and me a chance to catch up."

"Just say when," Katie replied.

What're you doing tomorrow night at about 6:30ish?" Jane asked. She raised her eyebrows towards me as if to ask if it was okay.

"Sure thing," I nodded.

"How about if I order some pizza and we meet here at my apartment?"

"That's a good idea," Katie answered. "When I get there, I have something to tell you about Sam. It's too long to go into, but I think you'll find it interesting."

"Sounds good, Jane replied. "I shall see you then..."

Katie waved as she said goodbye, and we waved back.

"Of course, we'll spend a lot of time talking about what we all used to do together. I think it will be beneficial to you. I am looking forward to what she has to say about Sam too."

I nodded and smiled.

"I'm looking forward to meeting her and learning more about what we all did together. Maybe she has some insight on why Sam acted the way he did."

We woke up the following day. I stayed the night, but there was a lot of tension. There was no lovemaking, but we held hands until we went to sleep. The stress was still there, but we were very polite, and when I left for the Shelter, I kissed her on the cheek just before going out the front door.

"See you tonight?" Jane asked.

"Of course."

Chapter 17

When Jane got home after work at 5:45 pm the next day, I hadn't arrived yet. I was finishing updating the shelter to make sure everything was running smoothly. Before I left, Reverend Myers called, and we talked. He told me that things were stable with his sister for the time being. During the conversation, he must have detected that something was bothering me.

"Is everything okay with you, Ken?"

"Not really. I've started remembering certain things, but I got a real shock yesterday. I found out that when Jane broke things off with me the second time, she had regained her memory just a few days after her accident. She lied to me. Her mother accidentally let the cat out of the bag."

"So, what are you going to do?

"I don't know yet. We're getting together tonight to meet with a mutual friend. Her name is Katie, and she has information that might jog my memory. I think I'm going to hold off from making any decisions about Jane for now. She has helped me a lot through all of this. After I regain more of my memory, I will have to decide if I'm going to stay with her."

"Hmm. I hope this doesn't mean you're going to use Jane and then dump her."

I wasn't used to hearing that kind of feedback from Reverend Myers, and it surprised me. After a few seconds, I answered, "I hope you don't think of it that way."

"My heart seems to remember some hurt from the past. I think it must have been very significant. I don't want to get so attached and get hurt again."

"May I speak my mind?"

"Of course!"

"You have to make your own decisions Ken. Both of you have lied to each other, and you both have been through a lot. But when I see how the two of you look at each other, I think that the attachment you're trying to avoid has already happened."

Reverend Myers was right. The emotional bonding had already occurred. But was I afraid, and I felt vulnerable.

"I see your point. I'm going to think about it some more and decide what to do next."

"The last thing I'll say is this. I think Jane is in love with you and she would be good for you. She seems like a good person and has your best interests at heart. But you have to make your own decisions. I'll always support what you decide."

I smiled. "You have been an incredible friend to me. Thank you for your advice."

"I'll see you when I get back."

We hung up, and I left the shelter. Reverend Myers had become a mentor to me during the worst time of my life. I had a lot to think about. He had shared some important observations.

On the way to Jane's apartment, I stopped at Kentucky Fried Chicken and bought a bucket with some biscuits, mashed potatoes, green beans. While I was paying for it, I received a text message from her asking where I was. I answered that I was only 10 minutes away. When I arrived, I knocked on her apartment door. She opened it almost right away and took a deep whiff, and smiled, "I smell supper."

I looked towards the kitchen and watched Jane finish setting the table in the dining room. She smiled and moved towards me. We embraced and kissed. "Let's eat," she said. "Katie will be here in about an hour."

I went to the bathroom and washed my hands and kept thinking about what Katie was like. But I still couldn't get Jane off my mind. My feelings for her were very intense but confused.

I now remembered Katie's face but not much else. Still, I felt very hopeful about her visit.

While we ate, we caught up with the day's events, and there seemed to be less tension. I had checked my cameras a few times during the day, and there was nothing unusual.

At 7:15 pm, there was a knock on the door. Jane looked through the peephole.

"It's Katie," she said as she opened the door. Katie had brought a 6-pack of Budweiser beer. When she got inside and saw me, she raised the beer towards me and said, "I brought your favorite, and it's cold."

I stared blankly in her direction.

"It is?"

"Oh yeah, sorry. I forgot you don't remember."

She then put the cans of beer on the dining room table, grabbed one, and then turned and hugged me.

"It's good to see you, Ken."

"I vaguely remember you."

"Well, I hope I can help you to remember more," she smiled.

Then she walked to the empty easy chair facing the sofa and plopped down, placing her beer on the coffee table, all in one motion.

Jane took one of the beers and took the rest to the refrigerator in the kitchen. When she returned to the couch, Katie told me that she thought I looked good.

I recognized her, and it made my mind race like a computer trying to locate lost data. I nodded my head and said, "Thanks for offering a beer, but I'm not going to drink any alcohol until it's safe and my memory comes back."

"I understand," she nodded.

I got up, went to the kitchen, and opened the refrigerator. I returned with a Coke Zero. I liked Coke Zero so much I was sure it was my past choice of soft drinks. When I snapped the ring at the top, pressure caused some of it to gush onto my lap, and we all laughed. The laughing seemed to release some of the stress. I reached for a napkin from the coffee table and dried it as much as I could.

After Jane opened her beer, Katie toasted me and declared, "We have some catching up to do."

"I agree". I have a lot of questions," I replied as I began sipping my drink.

"I'm sure you do," Katie smiled. "But first, take a look at this." She handed me a photo of Sam, Jane, Katie, and me together at the trailer where she and Sam lived. Both Jane and Katie studied my face without speaking.

I stared at it silently for several minutes, looked up at them, and then stared at it again. After a few minutes, I took a deep breath. Memories were flooding my brain like a giant waterfall. I had to shake my head a couple of times.

"I remember this. It was at... Sam's... trailer?"

"Yes!" Jane yelled.

I couldn't stop looking at the photograph. The more I looked at it, the more my past rushed in. It filled in the empty spaces that had left me lost in a maze of an unfamiliar world. It was a lot to take in. Strong emotions overtook my body, and memories of the past almost took my breath away. It was like all the pieces of my puzzle had all come together at the same time. I looked away from the photograph and then rested my forehead on the palms of my hands. After a few minutes, Katie and Jane looked at me and then at each other with amazement as I began to cry.

Jane put her hand on my shoulder to comfort me.

I rubbed my face up and down and then rubbed my eyes vigorously.

"I remember almost everything now," I said.

My emotions were jumping back and forth from joy and fear. I also I remembered what happened the day I was drugged.

I looked at Jane and Katie and said, "That night when everything happened, I had gone to a party after a performance in Corrales. I didn't know the guy who invited me, but he seemed very friendly."

I stopped again as things were quickly coming back.

"We kept going over our history up until we had stopped seeing each other. We laughed loud and often as we reminisced over funny things that we had done together. There was a lot of gossip about Sam and his new girlfriend too. I was almost afraid to stop for fear I might lose my memory again, and I kept thinking about how I needed to meet with Jim and tell him the story about my night of horror.

I remembered the night of the assault vividly now. It seemed like a small party of a few guys drinking at a house I had never been to before. I left the apartment that night because I was feeling sick. I had to walk to my car, which was parked almost a block away. I was dizzy and felt like I was going to pass out. As I approached my car, someone grabbed me from behind and threw something over my head so I couldn't see. At least two men threw me to the ground and started punching me. They held me down, and I remember struggling, kicking, and punching, but they were too strong. They pushed me into a car, and someone punched me in the face, causing me to lose my balance. Then I felt the car moving and heard their voices, but after a few minutes everything went black. The voices had Mexican accents. The next thing I knew, I was upside down in the car with a massive headache. I never saw the two men. But I think Sam was also there by then. I was partly conscious, and he was looking at me through the window. Sam looked shocked like he didn't expect to see me. He put his index finger over his mouth, signaling for me to keep quiet. Then he disappeared, and everything went blank.

After sharing the information, I stopped and shuddered, covering my mouth as I relived the terrifying events. I had a panic attack. It was like going through the horror right at that moment. I had trouble breathing.

Jane recognized my distress and tried to hug me as I shook, but I pushed her away.

By then Jane and Katie were in shock and didn't know how to respond. They kept looking at each other and then back to me.

I moved back from Jane and fixed my eyes on her. I must have had a scary look on my face.

"What are you thinking about?" she trembled.

"I am having a hard time handling all of this. It was awful. I can't understand why they would do that to me. What the hell did I do to them? What the hell did I do to Sam?"

"I can't imagine," Katie responded.

"Do you want to call Reverend Myers?" Jane asked.

"No, I don't think it would help right now."

We all sat quietly for some time, occasionally looking at each other, while Jane and Katie looked helpless, waiting for some sign from me so they could help.

I was now starting to put every detail into perspective. It was like a door had opened, and all the memories had knocked me down. They were jumping up and down on my brain.

Then my thoughts began to shift, and I felt sorrow.

"Now I remember when you got into your accident when we broke up, how we got back together, and then how we broke up the second time," I recalled.

Jane didn't respond, but she looked frightened.

I was feeling both anger and relief over what I had remembered. Jane had been pretty ruthless the day she demanded that I leave her house and not come back. It had caused a lot of pain for me.

Jane and Katie were now looking at each other as if they didn't know what to do. Silence filled the room and became unbearable for Jane.

"Are you ok?"

Our eyes met, and I then looked down at the floor and stopped talking.

Jane seemed unnerved over my reaction to the break-up. Her expression was both apprehension and sadness.

After a few moments, I recovered enough to ask more questions about Sam and what Katie knew about him. She assured me that she hadn't talked to Sam for a long time and her most recent information was from what she had learned from Becky.

I kept thinking about how Sam was something like Judas. But I also wondered what I had done to him. Maybe the other men made him think Ken and Kelly were the same and had crossed them in some way.

Then I smiled. I now realized that. I had never been involved in criminal behavior and would never break the law by hurting others.

Jane recognized the reaction and hugged me for several seconds before trying to kiss my lips, but I turned and pulled away.

"I'm sorry I didn't give you a chance after my accident," she cried. "It doesn't matter anymore," I answered.

"Yes, it does, and you know it," she sobbed.

She was right. It did matter. I remembered everything now, including the pain and heartbreak I had suffered from the breakups. I remembered crying. And I wasn't the type that cried. But I didn't want to talk about it now.

After Katie regained her composure, she changed the subject. "How well do you remember Sam now?"

But Jane interrupted, "Wait! First, tell us about your brother, Kelly."

I looked down. "I never knew of him unless I still can't remember that part. I can't understand why my parents wouldn't tell me about him."

I thought about it for a few more seconds. "My dad was a twin. He was always talking about how hard it was for him and his brother. It caused them problems at home and school. But he never went into any detail. His twin brother had been murdered when they were younger adults. My father couldn't afford to go to his funeral because it was in another state. It bothered him. It was when I was young, and we were poor and lived from one day to the next. It was a bad time for us. I may not ever know much else about my family. Now that I think of it, I have an aunt in Colorado who probably knows. But I haven't spoken to her since I was a child, and it will take a lot of time trying to find her. At least I hope ..." I shook my head vigorously, trying to remember.

Then I stood up. "I don't know about Sam. I hadn't seen him for a good while. He was a real asshole towards me."

"Do you remember when you and he had the argument, and he ran you out of his house?"

"Yes, I do. I was pissed! He said some pretty shitty things! I think his new girlfriend had something to do with it. She had a lot of influence on him."

Jane then asked, "How much do you remember about Becky?"

"The closest I ever got to her was that day of the argument. I never saw her, but I knew she was in the bedroom. Sam was impulsive, and I know he liked her. I felt like she was manipulating him. When he said all those things, I think she was listening. I think she orchestrated the whole thing."

"Well, it sure sounds like Becky," Katie replied. "She just called me out of the blue yesterday, asking if I knew where he was."

"Who the hell cares?" I replied sarcastically. "Maybe he had a new flame!"

"Maybe so," Katie replied. "But Becky seemed pretty worried. She said she thought Sam might have called me. I admit that it felt like Becky was getting a taste of her own medicine. She had been very catty towards me. She rubbed it in that he chose her over me more than once. She implied that Sam told her that when you two went with those two women, it had been your idea."

I laughed, "That sounds just like him. He's a weasel." Then I thought about it some more.

"I don't care about that part of Sam anymore. He was and is a liar. I only care that he gets what is coming to him for his involvement in my... attempted murder... which reminds me, I have a lot to tell Jim."

Jane interjected, "I never thought the cheating was your idea either, but I was disgusted with what you did. You have to own that."

"I know. But I remember taking responsibility for it."

"That's true."

"I think I need to call Jim and Reverend Myers and let them know about what I have remembered too. I also should call the Dr. who treated me for this. He'll be glad, and Jim will have more information about the night that I was abducted... and Sam."

I shook my head. "I'm so relieved that I am starting to remember everything... and that I'm not some asshole criminal. But it's a lot to handle."

At that point, we agreed to stop talking about it. For the rest of the evening, we talked about things they had done together in the past. I was amazed at how much I was remembering. I felt a sense of sadness though, because most of my family was gone, and I never got to meet my twin brother. But at least I didn't feel lost anymore. I had some old friends and had made some excellent new ones.

But I was also troubled. I couldn't shake the memory of the hurt surrounding the breakups with Jane. I couldn't deny that it had changed my perceptions of "us" either. I wasn't sure what to do next because I felt vulnerable and needed some time to decide what to do.

Katie seemed to sense that Jane and I needed to talk privately, so she said she had to go. As she left, she agreed to let us know if she heard anything else from Sam or Becky. She was happy to help me restore some of my memory. I felt deep gratitude towards her.

I stayed awake for a few hours, going over everything I remembered. My throat was dry, and my head was hurting, so I went to the kitchen to get some water and take some aspirin. When I looked around the kitchen, I noticed the bat and was suddenly reminded about its significance.

Before I graduated from high school, another student who was a star football player, had bullied me unmercifully. He was jealous because his girlfriend had taken an interest in me. He always made sure that he belittled me in front of other students and his girlfriend. I was terrified and mad at myself for being so weak.

I was so frightened that I took a self-defense course from a judo instructor with the hopes of overcoming my fears. He taught me how to use the bat to defend myself, and I was thankful for that, especially now that I might still be in some danger. While it helped me learn some techniques, it had done more to help me build confidence, but I still didn't know how I would react if someone attacked me.

What would I do if attacked? Would I fall apart? I hoped I would never have to find out.

Chapter 18

I contacted Reverend Myers after Katie left and told him the good news about my visit with Katie and Jane. He was very pleased and assured me that God was watching over me. He asked how things were going at the Shelter, and I guaranteed that everything was going well. After his return, we agreed to meet for breakfast to update him regarding the Shelter and my good personal news.

I then attempted to contact Jim, but there was no answer. I left a message giving general information about regaining my memory and Sam.

Jane and I stayed up until midnight talking about our relationship and the pain we both had suffered from it. But Jane was quieter and let me take the lead. She recognized that I was more distant and guarded. The more we talked, the more I recalled more things about it. It was a very emotional experience because, despite all the hurt, the feelings we had for each other were strong. If I decided to continue with her, it would be challenging to go through another breakup. I had lost some confidence in my future with Jane, but my feelings left me in turmoil.

We eventually focused on what I remembered about my experience the night of the abduction. There were still some missing pieces. What possible reasons could anyone want to hurt me? I couldn't recall anyone that could be that mad at me. There was one key event that I remembered that was crucial to the incident. I remembered what Sam had once told me about when he had gone home with a girl he met at a bar and spiked her drink with a drug to relax her so she would have sex with him. When he saw that I had gotten upset about it, he said that he hadn't used very much of it, and the girl was fully aware of what was going on. He promised he would never do it again. Sam's account made me believe that he was the one who had spiked my drink with Ketamine. But I didn't remember seeing him at the party.

By then, Jane was emotionally exhausted. She was happy that my memory had returned, but her concern about our relationship was evident. There was a lot to think about for both of us.

Jane also knew that if someone had tried to kill me before, they might try again. But she was convinced that my danger started with mistaken identity. When we went to bed, there was an awkwardness, and I couldn't sleep. I just kept looking up at the ceiling and worrying about the future. It wasn't just about Jane. It was about finding out if the reason I almost got killed. Could Sam have been fooled too?

At about 2:00 am, Jane turned to me and asked if I was okay. I assured her that I was, but she persisted. She couldn't sleep either.

"Yes, but are you okay with "us?" I was quiet for a few minutes before answering.

"I think everything will be okay. But I need some time to sort things out. When my memory returned, so did the hurt and heartbreak. I don't think I could go through that again."

She touched my hand with hers and said, "I understand, but I love you. We've been through more than most couples go through in a lifetime, and here we are."

"Yes, here we are. But we're not in the same place as yesterday. I need time."

"Of course," she said. "I'll give you some space, but please talk to me and let me know what's happening with you." Then she took a deep breath and closed her eyes.

I didn't sleep, and I don't think she did either. I kept going over the events of my abduction. I kept envisioning the men who were peering through my windows at night and my breakup with Jane. It was a lot to handle.

What stuck out about Jane was when we parted. Jane had said some very insulting things to me. She had told me I was a selfish son of a bitch and looked disgusted when she demanded I leave her home immediately and told me to never come back. I kept seeing the image of the anger and what seemed like hatred in her eyes, but I also remembered what Reverend Myers had said. He was right about my strong emotional attachment to her. Even if I chose to leave her, I would still be hurt again...a lot!

The following day, we got up and had coffee and cinnamon pop tarts. Neither of us said much, but there seemed to be less tension. Before I left, we hugged for a long time, and I kissed her on the lips. She looked at me with a searching glance, and I reassured her that everything would work itself out. The reality was that I loved her but was scared. The dilemma dominated my thoughts, and I knew it was going to be challenging to move forward.

When I arrived at work, I immediately helped the serving line for the homeless men and women. The mood was cheerful, and there were no arguments. It helped me keep my mind off Jane. Once I finished the cleanup, I poured a cup of coffee and put some creamer and sugar in it. I kept stirring it and was deep in thought about everything that had happened to me. As I stared off into space, Reverend Myers came and sat next to me.

"How are you, Ken?"

"I'm okay, but I hoped when my memory returned, it would be a total relief, and everything would be positive and back to normal. It's much more complicated. I'm worried about my safety, and now that I have the full memory of what happened between Jane and me, everything seems upside down. I hadn't remember that she had broken my heart so badly."

"I can see your point. Have you made an appointment with your doctor?"

"I decided that I'm not going to talk to any doctors about this. I want to work it out for myself."

"It's up to you, but you have been through a lot. You might want to reconsider."

Reverend Myers was studying me now.

"So, where do things stand with you and Jane? She has been supportive, and it's obvious to me that she cares deeply about you."

"I know that. But Jane also was ruthless when she broke up with me the second time. She said I was a selfish son of a bitch, yelled at me to 'get the hell out! I have to think about it some more."

Reverend Myers nodded and said, "Of course it's up to you. Based on what you've told me about the situation, she had a head injury and felt pressured by you. She might not have been herself. And that's the last thing I'll say about it. But make sure you consider that."

"Of course, I will. It's just painful."

At that moment, I heard Jim's voice behind me. He put his hand on my shoulder and shook me. When I looked up at him, he had a broad grin on his face.

"Sounds like you're making real progress, Ken.

"Yes, I am," I nodded.

"Do you think we can discuss what you remember about the abduction?" "Absolutely!"

"Let's go for a ride and just talk."

"That sounds good to me... let's go."

Reverend Myers looked at me and said, "Go! Don't worry about the shelter. Jim is more important."

We went to Jim's Unit and left the shelter immediately. I told him everything as we drove around the nearby neighborhood. I was sure that it was Sam's voice I heard during the abduction. I also told him about when Sam used a drug with the girl he met at the bar.

"I need to find Sam and question him. Do you have any idea where he might be?"

"I have no idea. According to his ex-girlfriend, she was worried because she hadn't seen or heard from him for days. If anyone knew how to reach Sam, it would be her."

"Do you have either of their phone numbers?" "No, but Katie does."

"Okay, I'll call Jane and get Katie's number. I may be a little slow right now because I am working on two other cases, so don't be surprised."

"I understand."

"By the way, how is the dog hunting going?"

"I haven't found one yet. It'll probably take a while, and I'm not in a big hurry. I'm not sure I want that responsibility right now. Everything is moving so fast. Besides, Jane has a dog that is with her a lot of the time."

"Well, I'm glad you have Jane. She can help you a lot. She cares about you."

"About that...things are a little shaky right now. When my memory came back, it also brought back how we broke up. It was a lot worse than I expected. She said some things that make me wary."

"Well, she gives me good vibes and has been very helpful in all of this. I hope you can see that."

"I do, but..."

"Have you thought about seeing a doctor to discuss all of this? You're going through a lot. You might have PTSD."

"I might, but I am going to try to work it out for myself first."

"Well, let me know if you need anything. If nothing else, you've proven to be pretty stubborn," he laughed. "In the meantime, I think Sam is our best chance of getting to the bottom of what happened to you. If he participated, he knows everything about why he or someone else wanted you dead. He might be thinking you already remember everything and is on the run."

"I hadn't considered that. You might be right."

"Do you think he got involved because he thought you were Kelly?"

"I've been thinking about that. Mistaken identity is the only thing that makes sense to me, and I think he wouldn't have participated in something like that unless he was being pressured by someone else or others. As mad as I am at him, I don't think he's a murderer."

Jim brought me back to work, and when I arrived, Jane had texted me to ask where I was going after work. I didn't answer but felt sick and anxious.

At the end of the workday, I drove home and stopped in the driveway. I checked around the house and the security clips on my phone. Everything was normal. After checking my mail, I sat down on my easy chair and closed my eyes. I was so tired that my body sunk into the chair. But my mind was on Jane. As hard as I tried, I couldn't stop thinking about her. I was filled with anxiety and couldn't stop stressing about it. Finally, I dialed her on my cell phone. After a few rings, she answered.

"Hello?"

"Hi Jane, it's me."

It was quiet for a few moments before Jane asked, "How are you?"

"I'm better, but I can't stop thinking about you."

"So, how are we?" she asked.

"I think we're going to be okay. We should have a serious talk. How about tomorrow night at my place?"

"Uh... you know I'm on my cell phone, right?" she asked.

"And?"

"I was actually on my way to your house right now. It's Friday, so I took a chance that you might want to see me and talk. I'm about a mile away from you right now. I hope that's okay. But if you want, I can go back to my apartment."

"No, now that I think about it, there is no point in delaying things. Let's do it."

I felt vulnerable but was ready to talk about it. I made some iced tea and poured two glasses.

When Jane arrived, we hugged and sat at the dining room table, making small talk. We ordered pizza. At first, things were a little awkward, but we finally looked at each other, and the challenging discussions were about to begin.

Chapter 19

It was Friday afternoon, and Sam was glad to be away from Albuquerque. He decided he would never go back. There were too many demons, and he was sure he had some dangerous enemies who would probably kill him if they could find him. It was sad that he had to end the relationship with Becky so abruptly, but he felt safer where he was and was sure he had done the right thing. He regretted not having told her face-to-face but felt like his life was in danger and didn't want to give any clues about where he was going. He needed a fresh start and had learned from some of the bad mistakes he had made in Albuquerque.

One of his biggest mistakes was selling drugs for Juan, especially heroin. It wasn't a small operation. Juan was already putting pressure to do more so he could control Sam. Worse, Sam had been skimming from some of the drugs he was delivering. He was worried that Juan may have discovered it. At first, he had thought he could get away with it because he wasn't taking much, but now he realized that a precise accounting system was in place. Juan had proven that he checked everything meticulously and was a violent enforcer.

Sam was sure that no one knew about his cousin Chris, who lived in Texas, not even Becky. Since his last name was Glew, he figured that no one connected them as cousins.

Chris was happy that Sam was coming to stay with him. His rent was high, and if Sam decided to stay there, it would ease the pressure and there was plenty of room for both of them in his rented house. Life would be more exciting too because Sam knew how to have fun. He always brought drama and women into the lives of those around him. He was also a good source of weed. Chris was only an occasional user of marijuana, but he didn't have any good contacts. Sam did. But Chris had no idea about how deep Sam was in the drug scene.

When Sam arrived at his cousin's house, Chris was standing outside his door. He was a little older than Sam and 6'1". He was heavier than Sam too, but not as athletic. He was dressed in jeans, and blue polo shirt, and some inexpensive blue ACICS tennis shoes. He was reasonably good-looking despite being overweight but didn't have the confident look that Sam did.

Chris's house was a single story sandy colored adobe style structure. It had rusty-colored shingles on the roof, and it was in an older neighborhood with similar houses on each side of the street.

Sam parked next to Chris's in the driveway and saw him standing outside his open door. He waived to him while he was getting out of his car. As he approached, Chris yelled, "Hey man, how was the drive?"

"Smooth," Sam replied. "I couldn't get away from there fast enough."

After a brief hug, Chris guided Sam through his house and showed him his bedroom. The home was sparsely furnished, and there was one 32" screen TV in the living room. Chris' bedroom had a small separate bathroom so Sam could use the one in the hall leading to his. Chris confided that he wasn't going to tell his landlord about Sam because he would raise the rent. This arrangement would be easier for both of them. If the landlord ever questioned him about Sam, he would say that Sam was visiting from Albuquerque. By the time the landlord would figure it out, Chris would know if he would stay long-term.

Since Sam had left Albuquerque so abruptly, he didn't have an extra set of clothes or personal hygiene items. He had some money from his job to buy just enough to get by until he could find a job in Amarillo. He didn't tell Chris, but he knew that he would get a place of his own once he found a job and built some savings. In the meantime, it was only fair to help with the rent. They talked about it briefly, and Sam agreed to start paying $400.00 a month, beginning the following month. Basic utilities were included in the rent.

After finishing the guided tour, Sam and Chris sat and started drinking Chris's favorite beer, Dos Eques. After the second beer, Sam told why he left Albuquerque. When he started talking about his relationship with Juan, Chris nodded slowly, and his expression changed.

"The dude sounds rough."

"He's dangerous, but there is no way he knows anything about you or your address."

Then Sam told him a story that shocked him and triggered more fear by Chris.

"Becky introduced me to Juan, a friend of her family. Juan and Becky's father became close. Juan gave me a job as an apprentice plumber since I didn't have any certification or license for plumbing as a favor to Becky. It provided great pay. I thought I had hit the lottery. The pay was generous, probably because of Becky, and was far more than I have ever earned before. It would have paid almost $50,000 a year, which is incredibly high for an apprentice. That should have been a red flag."

Sam took a deep breath.

"During our breaks at work, Juan would share weed with us and even other drugs if we wanted it."

"What kind of drugs?" Chris asked.

"Cocaine, heroin... you name it."

Understanding the gravity of the situation, Chris asked, "Are you sure they don't know where I live?

"I'm sure! Becky only knows I have a cousin in Amarillo but nothing else!"

Sam still didn't seem wholly convinced but took Sam's word.

"Juan was happy to hear that I had sold some weed from time to time. He said he sold a lot drugs and asked if I would be willing to sell for him. He said he would give me a cut and that his friends would look out for me. Like a dumbass, I agreed. I was nervous, but I sold weed in kilos and some cocaine."

Chris shook his head.

"That was dumb as hell!"

"Then Juan had his hooks in me and started ordering me to start selling heroin. That's when I realized he was in a gang or some big operation. He had some high rank in whatever he was part of. But that wasn't the of it. He made me start participating in roughing up some other gang members. That's not my style, so I told him that I didn't want to participate. He made it clear that he owned my ass and that I would be sorry if I didn't do what he said. He even punched me out for standing my ground."

Chris cringed. "Damn!"

"I honestly don't know how deep he is."

"Anything else I need to know?" Chris asked as he fidgeted uncomfortably in the easy chair.

"Well, yeah," Sam stuttered. "Once Juan knew he had me trapped, he ordered me to go with one of his gang members... a guy named Hector, to dispose of a drug dealer who was stealing from him. He was an identical twin of a friend of mine. It was bizarre. I didn't have to do much except go with him, help subdue him and roll him off a cliff in the mountains."

"That's murder!"

"No, attempted," Sam replied. "He lived, but the news reported it as an accident and said that he had amnesia. We had the wrong twin too. We fucked up! Because he was still alive, Juan told us that we weren't finished. We had to get rid of Ken before he got his memory back, so we had a little chase of our own going on. I tried to convince Juan that Ken didn't see who we were, and it was unnecessary, so he got rough with me and told me that I was going to help clean up the mess or else. He said there were too many loose ends and that this was a way for me to prove my loyalty. It was obvious that if it were that easy for him to kill, my life would be over if I didn't cooperate."

Chris started to worry again. "Are you sure that none of your friends know about me and my relationship with you?"

"Hell no! Like I said, I told my girlfriend that I had a cousin that lived in Amarillo but didn't give your last name or your address. And your last name is different from mine. If I didn't think we were safe, I wouldn't have come here."

Chris leaned back in his chair and nodded. "This is pretty weird stuff. But I think the least you could do is go in halfers for an alarm system for this house."

"That's a good deal. I'm in for half! I'll make some calls in a couple of days and get one installed. Tomorrow I'm gonna buy some clothes and other things so I can keep clean."

Sam had learned from this terrible experience and wanted to leave it behind him. But he wasn't as confident as he had portrayed to his cousin.

That night, Sam turned in early. He was exhausted from the day's work and long drive. For the first time in weeks, Sam didn't have the anxiety that had plagued him for recent weeks and slept soundly. When he woke up the following day, Chris was getting ready to go to work. The house smelled like toast, fruit loops, and coffee.

"I left some coffee for you on the counter. You can eat anything you can find," Chris called out as he went out the front door. I left you my only key. Don't lose it!"

"Catch ya later," Sam replied. He grabbed the key next to the door and looked out the window. Then he watched his cousin get into his silver 2006 Tacoma and drive out of the parking lot.

After two slices of toast with strawberry jam and two mugs of coffee, Sam took a shower and put his musty clothes back on. He then found some spray deodorant in his cousin's bathroom and sprayed his underarms and all over his clothes. Now he smelled like Right Guard. It was still an improvement. Next, he locked the door and got into his truck. He drove to the Super Walmart just a few blocks away and started shopping. He bought some reasonably priced clothing that would be enough for three changes of clothing and grooming items. He added some groceries to do his share of the cost of living with his cousin. He added a case of Dos Eques as well. The price for all of it was over $200, which was a lot, but still a bargain. He then stopped at a Wendy's across the street from the Walmart and ate a Dave's Single Burger with fries and a Coke. While he was there, his cell phone rang. When he pulled it from his pocket, he saw Becky's name on the screen, with her image. He immediately turned his phone off and put it back in his pocket. He knew she would stop trying to reach him eventually. Responding to her would allow anyone to track him to his location, including the police. He decided it would be a good idea also to change his phone number.

When Sam returned to Chris's apartment, he put the groceries away and changed into a new pair of Wrangler Jeans and a light blue short-sleeved Wrangler shirt. Then he changed from his running shoes to leather sandals and hung up his new clothes in the closet of his room, grabbed a Dos Equis, and settled into soft cushions of the living room couch. He reached the remote from the glass-topped coffee table in front of him and punched the buttons until he was tuned to the local news. As he watched one bad news story after the other, he sipped on the beer until it was empty. He must have still been tired because he drifted into a deep sleep. When he awakened, it was 2:00 in the afternoon. He looked around the apartment. There was no reading material anywhere. Unlike Chris, Sam liked reading when he wasn't high. He looked out the window for a long time and watched cars passing by. Then he texted Chris and asked for the password for his computer. Chris texted back, "screw123."

"Thanks... would you like for me to order pizza for tonight?" Sam asked.

"Sure, if you're buying."

"Don't worry. I got it. What time will you get back?"

"Around 5:30."

"I bought some beer. Let's party tonight!"

"Best idea of the day!"

He put the phone on the coffee table and watched a pre-recorded game between the Texas Rangers and New York Yankees. It was a good game with a lot of homeruns. At 4:30 pm, Sam went online and clicked on the Pizza Hut link. He remembered that Chris liked the "Meat Lover's Pizza." He ordered the large stuffed-crust pizza. They said they would get to his address within 45 minutes.

The pizza was late, but so was Chris. Sam gave the delivery woman $18.00 for the pizza and tip. He kept the container closed until Chris got there, at 6:00 pm.

Once Chris settled in, they ate the whole pizza and started drinking the beer. They decided right then that they were going to drink the entire case to celebrate Sam's arrival. Chris decided he would call in sick for work the next day. They laughed and joked, and Sam forgot about all his troubles, at least at that moment.

Since Chris didn't have any weed, the beer would have to do. They turned on Netflix, watched "Friday the 13th," stayed up, and watched 2 of the ten sequels. They laughed and threw the empty beer cans at a trash can but missed most of them. Empty cans were strewn all over the living room floor.

Chris was too drunk and naïve to see the gravity of danger Sam had brought to his home. When they finally finished the entire case of beer, Sam threw up twice before he passed out after stumbling to his bed. Chris had already passed out on the couch. The air smelled like a mixture of beer and vomit, and as usual, Chris hadn't checked the locks on the doors.

Chapter 20

Sam and Chris had consumed plenty of alcohol. They had gotten so smashed that they were as good as unconscious. Sam got up and urinated all over his shoes before staggering to his bed. His knees hit the edge, and he toppled over face down.

Music was blaring from Chris's sound system and but none of his neighbors were close enough to complain. Chris and Sam hadn't ever gotten that drunk together before.

Chris woke up at about 2:00 am and drank some water to curb the dehydration. His head was spinning, and he was nauseous. Once he drank a glass of water, he sped to the bathroom but didn't make it to the toilet. He threw up all over the bathroom floor until there was nothing left but dry heaves. When that stopped, he slumped back against the adjoining tub with his face against the wall. Eventually, the spinning in his head slowed down, so he struggled to his hands and knees and crawled back to his bedroom, leaving a track of vomit in his wake. After settling onto the bed, he reached for the trash can and pulled it towards him incase he started throwing up again.

Chris' eyes were bright red and sore. He turned to his side instinctively so he wouldn't aspirate if he started throwing up in his sleep. Just as he was getting comfortable, he heard his front door swing open and footsteps coming inside his room.

"Chris must be thirsty too," he laughed. "He can't even hold onto a glass."

He stretched his arms before shifting to a fetal position.

Suddenly, Sam's bedroom door swung open, and a dark figure quickly jumped on him. Sam was athletic but was so drunk his reflexes were slow to react. To make matters worse, the attacker was also firm and built like a football player. Sam fought back valiantly but was no match, especially when the second person came into the room. He didn't have a clue that Chris was already dead and laying on his bed with knife wounds in his torso and chest.

Sam hit the intruder in the nose with his head and heard him moan. He felt warm blood dripping on his forehead. But then the butt of a .9mm crashed against his chin and mouth. He felt his front tooth shatter and the fragments penetrated the inside of his lip like shrapnel from a grenade. He was barely conscious when he felt a pillow slam down on his face, cutting off his airways. He tried to scream, but his voice was muffled. His arms and legs flailed desperately. Now, his weak, muffled moans were fading from beneath the pillow. The intruder repositioned the pressure with his full body weight eliminating all the oxygen. Sam grew weaker and weaker as the intruder grabbed his arms, and a third one grabbed his ankles.

Finally, his movements slowed until he couldn't resist any longer. His body began to twitch, and his bladder released, leaving a wet pool of urine on the sheets beneath him. The intruder finally removed the pillow from Sam's face, and all that was left was a motionless corpse. One of the men stood over him for a few moments catching his breath and watching for any signs of life. He checked for a pulse in Sam's neck, and there was none.

After a few moments, they heard the distant sounds of sirens getting nearer.

Chris hadn't put up much of a fight in the other room. He wasn't physically strong, hadn't been exposed to much aggression in his life, and didn't know how to defend himself very well. Because he was drunk, he had no chance at all. When the three intruders joined together in the living room, they were all still breathing hard. They agreed to run from the residence immediately, but one of them had realized he had lost his cell phone. He told the other two to go and he would find the phone. He searched until the sirens got so close he had no choice but to leave.

After a few more frantic moments of searching for the phone he ran in a direction away from the noise of sirens. He could already see the flashing lights outside the front living room window and realized that escape would be difficult. He quickly ran out the back door but stopped abruptly when he heard a loud command right behind him.

"Freeze! Put your hands behind your head! Lie down on your stomach and cross your legs!"

Lights blinded him as two Amarillo police officers approached him carefully and frisked him. One of the officers removed a bloody knife and .9 mm from his belt. After handcuffing him the officers grabbed his arms from behind and stood him up. He could still taste the sand that had stuck to his lips and between his front teeth from when the officers had pushed his head down into the dirt while they cuffed him. They then escorted him to the front yard where there were three more police units. They placed him in the back seat of one of the units and cordoned off the crime scene. By now there were onlookers everywhere. He couldn't see any signs of the other two attackers though. After officers started searching the surrounding area, an officer returned to the unit he was in and he was eventually transported to the Amarillo Police station. Once there, he was interrogated before being booked into jail.

The Amarillo Homicide Unit of the Criminal Investigation Division (CID) was now combing through the crime scene of Chris Glew's residence. Both Chris and Sam's dead bodies were taken to the morgue after being pronounced dead. The Medical Examiner verified the cause of Sam's death as asphyxiation. Chris had died from lethal knife wounds to his liver and heart.

One of the neighbors had notified the police that they had heard glass breaking and a loud ruckus in Chris's residence.

The news media was now on the site and reporting that Amarillo City Police were investigating the crime scene. They reported that they were withholding the names of the victims until families could be notified.

Police convinced them to wait temporarily to report the identity of the man they had in custody until they had a chance to interrogate him to see who his accomplices were. The media reported that there was an ongoing search for the attackers who were armed and dangerous so the community would be appropriately warned.

The intruder wasn't talking. But when they checked, they learned his name was Jesus Maestas and he had a felony record of aggravated battery in the state of New Mexico. Since he was a convicted felon and armed with a .9mm he would be federally charged for being a felon carrying a firearm. He was also suspected of having connections with the Sinaloa Cartel in Mexico.

Not surprisingly, by the time law enforcement officers had gotten him into the interrogation room his attorney had intervened and told him to keep his mouth shut. Because of his history, the FBI and DEA had been contacted and were at the scene. During interrogation, they leaned on him pretty hard. Interrogators warned him about the seriousness of his crime and one officer leaned in whispering into Jesus's ear.

"It'd be a shame if it leaked that he had ratted." The officer was graphic when he reminded Jesus what would happen if other inmates heard that he was a snitch.

His attorney, John Salas was a public defender. He stood up next to Jesus and wedged himself between the officer and his client.

"What do you think you're doing? My client is not talking to you! I'll do the talking!"

When three more interrogators returned to where he was sitting, they read Jesus his rights and reminded him that if found guilty of murder in Texas he would almost certainly get the death penalty. They added that he was facing numerous federal crimes as well, including a felon in possession of a firearm.

Jesus flinched. He had been in prison before and had struggled before being paroled. But worse, a state conviction would be the end for him. If they leaked that he was a rat, he would die a horrible death anyway. Being tough outside of prison didn't always mean much inside those walls. Tough guys often turned into nobodies inside. Either way, he was facing death. He was panicked because he knew that no one inside the prison would protect him. Of the three intruders, he was the least experienced and weakest. He had always feared dying in prison or being killed by lethal injection in Huntsville.

Even with his Public Defender present, he had already softened up. His attorney, John Robinson, was young and had minimal experience, especially with a violent murder case.

When they were left alone, Jesus insisted on making a deal. Robinson finally agreed.

When the officers returned, Robinson asked them if they would offer Jesus a deal to avoid the death penalty and protection.

Detective Bob Santisteban was an experienced interrogator. He was six foot three and had a burly physique with a slight bulge in his midriff. He was wearing street clothes, but he had a Glock holstered to his belt on one side and a badge on the other. He was leaning across the table with his extra-large hands flat on the table staring at Jesus just a few inches from his face. He made it clear that Jesus had to give up the persons who were running the operation and his accomplices and if he did, they would recommend he be transferred to an out of state prison where he could get protection once convicted.

It had been surprisingly easy to break Jesus down. The continued reminders of the death penalty had paid off. They also agreed to work on getting him transferred out of state to do his time in protective custody if he cooperated. It meant he might even be able to avoid 23 hours a day of lockdown if transferred to the right facility.

But the other two killers, Gilbert Baca and Ramiro Gonzales were on the run. They had zigzagged through back streets and alleys until they had gotten to Jesus's unmarked business truck. Jesus had told them that if they got caught, to report the vehicle as stolen.

They quickly got into the truck and drove south through the town of Canyon Texas on highway 27 and then continued east on Highway 60 to Santa Rosa New Mexico. They didn't encounter any law enforcement vehicles on the road. From there, after stopping on the side of the road to take a quick bathroom break, they continued on I-40 until they reached Albuquerque. Gilbert contacted Juan and gave him a rundown on what had happened.

The hit was a close call, and their friend, Jesus Maestas, had gotten separated from them. He hadn't contacted them yet, but he was loyal. They were confident he would find a way out of Amarillo safely. They hoped he would contact them soon. They knew better than to contact him, in case he had been apprehended. The biggest worry was whether he had found the lost cell phone. If not, things would get complicated.

Either way, almost all the people who could connect them to Kelly Garrity's death were no longer a problem. There was only one left.

After Gilbert contacted Juan Perez, he and Ramiro disposed of their bloody clothes in a dumpster behind a Circle K away from their location and put on an extra set of clothes brought in case things got messy. He took Ramiro home, and they agreed to avoid discussing anything on the phone or meeting until they received more information. Ramiro and Gilbert agreed that Sam had put up a good fight, but that Chris was an easy kill. They hadn't thought they had left any evidence since they were wearing gloves. He didn't remember that one of them bled during the struggle, so he thought it would be hard to find any physical evidence. The only potential problem would be if Jesus was unable to find his cell phone and had left it at the scene. Now they had to wait until Juan contacted them.

Meanwhile, in Amarillo, the crime scene would be off-limits to everyone but Texas CSI for several days. They would thoroughly investigate any evidence there was, including forensics, to help solve the case. Soon, the press would write about Maestas and his involvement, so they had to act fast.

Investigators were trying to learn as much as possible before the media revealed their prime suspect to the public. Hopefully, they would learn a lot more from the cell phone numbers that appeared on the phone that they confiscated from the crime scene. One of the techs was already working on it. Jesus was cooperating for now but was being difficult regarding the phone. His clothes had been confiscated, and they expected to find Chris's blood on one of Jesus's shirt sleeves.

The Amarillo District Attorney's office was working closely with investigators on any deals offered to Maestas. He was being kept in segregation for his protection. Some inmates had already learned of his presence and wondering why he was segregated.

Detective Santisteban had Jesus escorted from his jail cell to a visiting room and handed him his cell phone.

"Contact your big boss," he ordered.

Jesus looked at the cell phone blankly and said, "I don't know his number."

Santisteban stared, tilted his head, and raised his eyebrows threateningly.

Jesus got the message. "Okay, okay…"

"You'd better say what I told you exactly, or the deal's off!"

Jesus dialed the number, and after several rings, he got an answer. "Hello?"

"Hello sir, this is Jesus. I'm just calling you to tell you I'm hiding but safe. We knocked off the two guys in El Paso. I got separated from the others, but no one knows where I am."

"What the fuck did you call me on this line for, you stupid fuck!"

"I didn't know what else to do. I couldn't reach anyone else, so I called you because I thought if I didn't, you guys would get pissed."

For the next ten minutes, Jesus kept answering that he would be coming back to Albuquerque as soon as things settled down and at one point, denied that the call was being recorded. Eventually, his voice became forceful, as if he was offended that he was being doubted. The person on the other end of the line was suspicious, but Jesus kept his composure until he completed the call with enough evidence for the Feds to move forward.

Chapter 21

I arrived at the shelter for work at 7:00 am. Reverend Myers said that he would be back the following day. I felt that if things kept going the way they had, I would have a great progress report for him. Everyone had pitched in, and the teamwork was phenomenal. They hadn't needed me there.

At 8:00 am, Jim called and apologized for the late callback. He had been out late on a homicide case. I filled him in on everything. We agreed that I should try to contact my aunt to see if she knew anything about Kelly. Jim stopped by the shelter at 10:30 am and said he was still following up on my case. He said that he had a few leads on Sam, but he appeared to be nowhere in Albuquerque. Again, he apologized that he was working on a new homicide case, wouldn't be able to give the amount of attention he wanted to my case but reminded me to call him immediately with any further information or if I thought I was in danger. After we finished, he patted me on the back and said, "You're gonna be okay."

"Thanks, man. I knew I would never be able to repay either you or Reverend Myers for all you had done for me. I appreciate all the help you've given me."

Jim smiled and opened the door. He turned before he left and waved. "Let me know if you hear anything that might help your case, okay?"

"I will."

During my lunch break, I received a call from Jane. She sounded nervous. She said that Katie told her that Becky had contacted her the day before. She told Katie that someone had gotten into her house and found a box she had packed with Sam's belongings. It was obvious that whoever it was, went through all of it and had left some of his things scattered around her bedroom. She guessed that it might have been Sam, since there was no forced entry, and he had a key. Becky asked Katie if she had heard from him. Katie told her she hadn't.

"What do you make of that?" Jane asked.

"I have no idea." Then I asked, "Did she know if anything unusual was missing?"

"If you want, I can ask Katie for Becky's number and call her back." I thought for a moment. "Sure, why not? What do we have to lose?" "Okay," She replied. "I am going to pick up my dog. I'll meet you at your house?"

"I'm not sure it's safe there."

"I think it'll be safe. We can't do everything out of fear. Besides, we have Bailey," she chuckled.

"Don't forget about the guys that were looking through my windows the other night. They might come back."

"Well, if we start to feel uncomfortable, we'll pack up and go to my apartment. Is that okay?"

"Alright, but I have to make sure everything is okay at the shelter first. I'll see you when I get done."

I got home at 5:45 PM. I found everything in order. I checked my mail and there was nothing but advertisements. I dropped them into the trash right after entering the house. Then I waited for Jane and decided to see if she would like to go out for dinner. I had been thinking of what Reverend Myers had said about Jane and me. He was right about all of it. Most importantly, he was right that I was already in deep emotionally with her. Admitting it to myself was actually, a relief. It made it easier for me to accept all the risks. I knew what I had to do.

Jane arrived at 6:40 PM. She was happy to see me and hugged me for at least a full minute. She was obviously tired.

"Don't get comfortable. Let's go out to eat at Teriyaki Express in Bosque Farms. I don't feel like cooking anything and I know you don't. If we go, we don't have to do anything but eat. Bailey can stay in my study. I'll leave him a bowl of water and put a blanket down for him."

Jane smiled, "You read my mind. I think Bailey'll be okay. He's pretty good about being left alone in my apartment and your house shouldn't be any different. He doesn't bother anything. Let's go."

After getting into my car we headed north to the restaurant. "Did you ever get ahold of Becky?"

"Yes, I did. She was mad because Sam is nowhere to be found."

"Sounds just like him."

"Yes," she said. "He works at a place called, Juan's Plumbing, on 98th Street, on the west side." She then looked up at the ceiling and said, "Sam sure pisses off a lot of people."

"You got that right, but we need to find him."

When we arrived at the restaurant, it was crowded. But the service was still very fast. Our meals were brought to our table in less than fifteen minutes. Mine was sweet and sour chicken and Jane had a stir fry of chicken with vegetables. As we ate, we talked for nearly an hour about what had happened to our relationship after her accident. She insisted that she wasn't herself when she demanded that I leave her house. She regretted lying and how she had reacted. She reminded me that she had had a brain injury and had been seriously injured.

"I was afraid about whether our relationship would survive."

"Nothing is totally certain Ken. Remember, this is scary for me too. I'll trust you if you trust me. But we'll have to be committed and be honest always. It was the lies that got us into trouble. There can't be anymore lies even when it's hard."

"I agree. The reality is I'm already in love with you, so there's no turning back."

Jane smiled, "Then we're both in the same boat. Let's row the boat."

I pulled her to me and kissed her. "Well, let's finish eating before our food gets cold."

When we finished, I paid the bill and left a 20% tip. We were both feeling drowsy from all the food as we drove back to my house. When

I parked my car in the driveway, I looked at her, and said, "One of the things I have always loved about you is your mischievous sense of humor. Everything has gotten so serious that I miss that part of you."

"You shouldn't have said that," she grinned. "That side of me will come back before you know it." Then she gave me a wicked smile.

Once we approached the house, I heard Bailey barking on other side of the door. Jane went with me as I circled the outside of the house. Everything appeared secure.

When I unlocked the door, Bailey started dancing around in circles and jumping up and down on Jane's leg. When she sat on the couch Bailey jumped on her lap licked her chin.

I took a tour of the inside of the house. Everything looked untouched so I returned to the living room. Jane and I settled into the couch and Bailey jumped onto my lap. He licked my face, and it took him a few minutes before curling up comfortably between Jane and me.

Within a few seconds I was kissing Jane on the neck and touching her breasts.

She turned towards me. "I thought you were tired."

I smiled. "Yes, but I 'm, not that tired."

"Let's try that later when we go to bed, okay?" She mumbled something, as her head snuggled her head on my chest. She was obviously sleepy.

I scrolled the TV channels with the remote until I found a Dateline episode. It was about a man who had killed and buried his wife in a wooded area 5 miles from his house. That wasn't the kind of thing I wanted to watch, so I changed the channel to the news. But it turned out to be background noise because we weren't really paying attention. Jane fell asleep with her head resting on my shoulder. In about ten minutes, all three of us were asleep. A short time after, I had to wake Bailey up because he was snoring. Then we went back to sleep. About an hour later I woke up with a start. Bailey had jumped off the couch and had run to the back door. I thought I had heard something outside the back door too.

Jane was sitting up and was looking at me, obviously frightened.

My heart was pounding with fear and my hands were shaking.

We checked the clips on from the cameras and were panicked when we saw nothing but black on the screen.

I whispered, "I think I heard some noise at the back door and so did Bailey. I'm going to check through the window. Get down on the floor behind the couch."

"I heard it too," she whispered. "Be careful and don't turn on the light. I'm dialing 9-11." She slid to the floor in front of the couch.

I was terrified as I tiptoed slowly through the kitchen picking up the bat next to the refrigerator and crept to the side of the door my heart was pounding because I wasn't sure I could handle an attack. I then carefully separating the blinds and was shocked to see another man's eyes staring right at me through holes of a black ski mask.

A gloved fist came crashing through the glass window and then the same hand reached in, unlocking the door, twisting the knob and pushing it open. I felt paralyzed, frozen and gripping the bat with all my strength. The sound of breaking glass caused Jane to scream and the beeping sound of the house alarm started to blare. Then a husky looking man entered with his gun drawn, followed by another man. They were both wearing masks. Jane screamed again and Bailey immediately ran and hid under the sofa. By this time, the alarm was shrieking unbearably and added to the chaos.

Jane continued to scream. She reached for her cell phone and dialed 911. Adrenalin was rushing throughout my body and I reacted with an explosion of energy. The first man through the door was pointing his handgun at me. Pure instincts caused me to hit his wrist with the bat with so much force that he squealed and dropped it. I was no longer thinking, just reacting. The intruder grabbed his wrist and pulled it towards his body as he shrieked from the pain. When the handgun bounced on the floor, it went off with a loud bang before careening off the wall. Jane screamed and then moaned. I impulsively hit the intruder as hard as I could in the middle of his face with a quick back handed blow with the bat. I felt the bones in his cheek crunching as he fell to the floor moaning with his hands covering his face.

I jerked my head up when I heard a loud clicking sound. The other intruder had tried to fire his weapon at me, but it had jammed. He stared at the weapon in disbelief and panic. When he started pulling on the top of the chamber, I quickly hit his hand with the bat as hard as I could. With a loud yelp, the intruder dropped his weapon, and grabbed his hand. The gun made a clattering sound as it landed on the linoleum in front of me. I kicked his weapon to the other end of the kitchen and lunged towards the other 9mm. The attacker swung his foot from behind me kicking my ankles with a sweeping motion, taking my legs out from under me. I fell to my hands and knees but frantically crawled towards the weapon. The attacker dove to the floor, grabbed my foot, so I kicked him in the face with my heel. I struggled forward reaching for the weapon, but he grabbed my foot again and twisted me onto my back. This time, I kicked him as hard as I could in the face with the heel of my foot. He let go and fell backwards but quickly regained his balance while I grabbed the weapon. He left his feet to dive on top of me, but by then I had pointed the gun at him. As he descended on me, I pulled the trigger and there was a loud bang that shocked my eardrums. The smell of burning gunpowder and smoke filled my nostrils as he yelped and collapsed on top of me. His weight was suffocating so I struggled to push his body to the side. Blood was everywhere on floor and all over the intruder and me.

The blaring house alarm was drowning out his cries for help. Once I was separated from him, I could see that the bullet had hit him right in the crotch area. No wonder he was screaming. By then, the other attacker was moving towards me. Still lying on my back, I pointed the gun in his direction with two hands, but my hands were shaking. I gripped the handle tightly to stop the shaking.

"Get on your fucking knees and put your hands behind your head! Any moves and I'll blow your fuckin brains out!"

I was so wound up I knew I could and would take his life if the situation called for it.

The intruder quickly got down on his knees and placed his hands behind his head. The whole side of his face was swollen, completely hiding his right eye and was already turning purple. His nose was broken and bleeding all over his shirt. He stared at me with a look of resignation, but I knew he would jump at any opportunity to get the gun away from me. By this time the other gunman was screaming louder than the house alarm for help as a pool of blood was growing beneath him. I yelled for him keep still and kept my eyes on both of them.

I yelled at Jane, 'Did you call 911?"

All I could hear from her was moaning and a gargling sound.

"No!" I gasped.

I struggled to my feet while keeping the barrel of the weapon trained on the two men. I leaned slightly over the back of the sofa so I could see her, and she was moving back-and-forth with a pool of blood next to her body. Bailey was whimpering and licking her face. At first, I panicked and couldn't think of what to do. My thoughts were disorganized, and I almost froze again.

I gritted my teeth and shook my head, determined to stay under control. I kept my eyes on both men as I pulled my cell phone from my pocket with my free hand and dialed 911. When the female dispatcher answered, I shouted over the alarm system. "Two men broke into my house and shot my girlfriend! I have them at gunpoint. I shot one of them and he's lost a lot of blood. My girlfriend is hurt bad and bleeding and might be dying! I can't help her because I have the attackers at gunpoint! Please hurry!"

I struggled to control my breathing and to avoid hyperventilating. I was trembling and suddenly felt exhausted. The relentless sounds of the house alarm were unbearable.

"Stay on the line!" She ordered. "We already received a call from your location and officers are on the way!"

I was finding it difficult to hold back tears, but my eyes were glued on the two men. The first attacker's forehead had a huge bump protruding at the top of his forehead. He looked at his partner and then back at me with a glare.

"Go ahead! Give me a reason!" I shouted and jerked the .9mm in his direction. By now, I was so angry, I found myself hoping he would make a move.

His body jerked and straightened, and his threatening stare changed to fear. The wounded man had lost a lot of blood, was quiet and had stopped moving. It was obvious he was starting to lose consciousness.

I slowly spelled the address to the dispatcher again, and she reminded me to stay on the line again. I was still breathing rapidly and was felt like I was starting to hyperventilate. By now, the alarm company was attempting to call me, but I ignored them.

By then, I could hear the faint sounds of sirens.

"Is she moving at all? Can you tell if she is breathing?" the dispatcher asked.

Yes, she's moving," I shouted desperately. "But she's hurt bad. Hurry!"

"Stay calm, and stay on the line," the dispatcher responded. "Help is within minutes from your location."

By then, I heard what sounded like several sirens outside the house. I could see red and blue lights flashing through the window. Two Valencia County Sheriff's Deputies, two Bosque Farms policemen, a Fire Engine, and Ambulance arrived. The sirens mixed with the house alarm was piercing the air, and flashing lights were everywhere. I heard more sirens in the distance. Two deputies banged on the front door and announced who they were. Two more local officers were at the back door. Their weapons were drawn, and they were looking right at the two assailants and me. I almost immediately heard Officer Montoya shouting to open the door.

"I have two intruders. One is wounded on the floor, and the other is on his knees in the kitchen. I have a handgun on them," I shouted in a broken voice. "My girlfriend has been shot and is on the floor in front of the couch! She's hurt really bad!"

"Is there anyone else in the house?"

"No, everybody is in this room!"

"We have officers at both entrances with their weapons drawn. Step away from the intruders and put your weapon down. Then put your hands up when I tell you, and we'll enter the house immediately."

My voice cracked as I answered, "Yes, sir!"

I slowly put the weapon down, and when I raised my hands, I yelled, "The weapon is on the floor!"

But all four officers were already storming through the doors with their weapons drawn. They ordered the conscious attacker to lie face down with his ankles crossed and hands behind his head. They cuffed him immediately.

Two more officers slowly checked the rest of the house to confirm that no one else was there.

Officer Montoya cleared the EMTs to join them after it was determined that no other occupants were in the house. One EMT attended to Jane and the other to the intruder who had been shot. One officer was already standing over him. He looked up at Officer Montoya and shook his head. "He's dead!"

One of the officers reached down and pulled the face masks off both intruders. He looked at me and yelled, "Do either of them look familiar to you?"

I turned my attention to Jane and the EMT who was administering first aid and stared at them. I don't recognize either one of them. Sorry. Can I turn the alarm off?"

"Yes! By all means!"

I keyed in the code twice, and the alarm stopped. Then I looked helplessly back at Jane.

Officer Montoya ordered me to move further out of their way. But I couldn't stop looking at Jane. The EMT working on her kept motioned me to stand clear.

"Is she gonna be okay?" I pleaded.

"I think she's gonna be fine. No vital organs were hit."

"Are you sure?"

"Nothing's for sure, buddy, but it looks encouraging right now."

I pointed one finger at the gunman, whose weapon had gone off when it hit the floor.

"His gun went off when it hit the floor after I knocked it out of his hand! The other weapon jammed, or both of us would probably be dead!" By this time, both EMTs were leaning over Jane, who was face-down on the floor. After checking her pulse, they slowly turned her over, and she let out a loud and painful moan. Her breathing was very rapid and she was gasping for air.

One of the EMTs looked at me and said, "I think she's going to make it, but one of her lungs appears to be punctured. We need to get her to the hospital right away."

They stabilized her and carefully lifted her onto a gurney with an IV inserted into her arm. She had stopped moaning by then.

I then gave my statement. I shared what I thought led to the attack, and Officer Montoya confirmed my story. He had already briefed the other officers.

After one deputy thoroughly checked the house for safety, the two officers who entered through the back door handcuffed the injured man, stood him up, and looked at me.

"You must've whacked him pretty good."

"That's what terror will do for you," I answered.

The entire property was cordoned off with crime scene tape and the Medical Examiner had arrived.

"What's your name?" one of the deputies asked the attacker.

He refused to answer as his menacing good eye stare trained on me.

The deputies removed the intruder and put him in the back of one of the units after the EMTs treated him. Once pronounced dead by the medical examiner, the body of the deceased attacker was zipped into a body bag, removed by ambulance, and taken to the morgue.

I asked if I could go to the hospital to be with Jane, but deputies told me they needed to finish getting my statement first. By then, I had gotten Bailey and kept him in my arms because he was still was shaking.

The Sheriff's unit transported the attacker to the Valencia County Jail. The remaining deputies were protecting the crime scene and combing the residence and property for evidence. Cameras were flashing as they made their rounds.

I contacted Jane's parents and told them that she was en route to Presbyterian Hospital on Central Avenue in Albuquerque and briefly explained what happened. They were shocked and horrified and told me they were going to meet me at the hospital.

Once the scene was secured, and the deputies had taken a complete statement, one of the deputies asked me if I was able to drive to the hospital. As a courtesy, Officer Montoya offered to take me. By then, I was calmer and told him that I could drive to the hospital on my own. I also wanted to have the freedom to go wherever I needed. He told me not to return to my home until the crime scene was cleared, which would take a few days. "Are you okay? I can get you in to see a doctor if you want. You've just been through a trauma, and don't forget that there might be more of them, so be very careful."

"Thank you, but I need to get to the hospital so I can find out how Jane is."

"Okay but take this ID card and call me if you need to see somebody," he said, as he handed me his business card.

The drive to the hospital wasn't easy. I couldn't stop trembling, and my thoughts were on Jane's condition. I couldn't help thinking the worst. It was probably pure luck that I made it to the hospital without having an accident. To make matters worse, knowing that I had just killed someone was making me nauseous.

When I arrived at the hospital, I immediately checked to see where Jane was, and the person at the front desk told me she was in surgery. He directed me to a waiting room in the surgery wing. He said the surgeon on the case was Dr. Phil Marshall, and he would let Jane's family know the outcome of the surgery.

When I entered the waiting room, Jane's father and mother turned and looked at me. Her father stood up and frowned, "What the hell happened?" He was worried and angry.

I had never seen him this way before. He had always been very calm, courteous, and friendly, so I backed away.

"She was staying at my house for the weekend, and there was a home invasion. Two thugs busted a window out on my back door and barged in. They had guns. I was lucky enough to overcome them. But Jane got hit by a stray bullet."

I kept having to add information because the trauma had disorganized my thinking.

Jack said, "In hindsight, you probably should have at least tried to keep her away. But when you look at how things developed with your amnesia and other things, I think it's understandable. We should just be grateful that things are okay for now. But you might still be in danger."

Jim nodded. "That's exactly right. We have a lot of work to do. This is not a local matter. The Feds are involved."

Finally, I was allowed to go in and see Jane. She was hooked up to monitoring machines and IV. I could see her heartbeat, oxygen level and blood pressure on the monitor. She had a mask, to assist breathing and a tube in her side to help drain fluids. She didn't appear to be in a lot of pain and was breathing steadily. She opened her eyes occasionally but didn't acknowledge anyone.

I watched her for several minutes and whispered in her ear, "You're going to be alright."

The nurse came into the room and reminded me that I was going to have to leave. She told me that Jane would probably be awake and responsive the following day. She urged me to go home to get some rest.

"How long will it take all of these wounds to heal?" I inquired.

"It was a clean wound and thankfully, the opening was small. Usually, it takes an injury like this, weeks to months, depending on whether there are complications."

I thanked her as I left and returned to the waiting room. Once I got there, I told her parents what the nurse had told me and said I was going to stay at the hospital. I knew I couldn't go home anyway. I said I would sleep in the chair.

Jane's parents urged me to go back to their house or Jane's apartment to spend the night. They convinced me that it would be better if we all went home and returned the next day. Jim seconded the recommendation, so I reluctantly left the hospital and headed to Jane's apartment.

Jim then warned me that if there were still others trying to kill me, they might know where Jane's apartment was by now. I agreed but told him that I felt safe enough alone in her apartment and if there was any danger, I was better off there than to put her parents in danger too.

As Jim left, he turned and said, "Don't hesitate to call if there is anything at all unusual. Okay?"

"I will be okay, I promise."

"By the way, you did a heroic act with those two thugs. It took a lot of courage to overcome those odds."

"Are you kidding? I almost had a heart attack with fear. I'll never get over it."

"Are YOU kidding? Everyone is terrified under those circumstances. We'll get you some help for the rest of it... and don't refuse it."

"Okay, I promise I won't."

I then turned and kissed Jane on the forehead before leaving the hospital.

Chapter 22

During my drive home from the hospital, the events during the attack at my home dominated my thoughts. As I entered Jane's apartment, I took a deep breath, closed my eyes, and collapsed on the couch. I wept uncontrollably for several minutes and couldn't stop trembling. The weight of the night's ordeal had finally taken its toll. After about 10 minutes, I sunk into the cushions and felt like I had no energy left. After about an hour, I could no longer fight the fatigue and fell into a deep sleep. My dreams returned to the physical encounter with the two assailants. I shook in my sleep when I considered how easily the outcome could have been different, with both Jane and me dead. My dreams had three different outcomes, and none of them were good. It was clear that someone wanted me dead, which meant I was probably still in danger.

I woke up with a start when my cell phone rang. It was Katie. I answered weakly, "Hello?"

"Hi Ken, is Jane there? Can I speak to her?" she asked.

"Katie, she's in the hospital. She's recovering from surgery and is at Presbyterian Hospital. Two guys broke into my house while we were there, and she got shot. I killed one of them, and the other one got arrested."

Hearing myself say that I had killed someone caused me to stop breathing for a few moments as the reality of it set in.

"Whaaaaaaat? Oh my God," Katie cried.

"She's going to be okay."

"Well, I have some more bad news," Katie said. "Sam and his cousin in Amarillo are dead. Becky called me and said they were murdered. No one has said exactly how they were killed, but they were brutally murdered. It's ugly."

"How did Becky find out?" I asked.

"Her phone number was on Sam's phone listed as 'ICE' as an emergency contact. She seemed very upset."

I panicked. "I need to call the sheriff's deputy who's been handling my case. I think I need protection and so, does Jane."

"This is too much," Katie shuddered. "I can't believe all this has happened. I agree that you probably need protection. I think someone is out to kill you, and it's probably because of your brother. They made a mistake and are now trying to shut you up."

"I agree," I need to make some calls. I'll keep in touch, and you do likewise."

After hanging up, I dialed Jim. Jim answered almost immediately. "What's up?"

I gave Jim a complete rundown on my conversation with Katie and asked if he could get some protection for Jane and me.

"I think you're safer staying at Jane's apartment. They have security there, and I will contact them and get them up to speed." Jim said. "Are you okay?"

"I'm happy with the arrest but not the killing. And I am terrified of Jane's condition because of it. I should have tried harder to talk her out of spending the night at my place."

"Hindsight is 20/20. But you did everything right and showed a lot of courage. Both of you are alive because of it. Killing someone is hard to cope with, and you'll probably need some professional help with it."

"So, What's next for you?"

"I'll let Albuquerque PD know about your situation so they can do more patrols in your area. I'm also going to talk with Valencia County about their investigation and learn as much as possible.

I'll keep in touch. I will also contact Amarillo PD and try to get more details on Sam and his cousin. Then I think I'll go pay Katie and Becky a visit."

"Thanks," I answered.

When we finished the call, I didn't feel safer, and I kept thinking about Jane and her current condition. I couldn't help wondering if it was partly my fault that she was injured. At least I wasn't being criticized by her parents, and most importantly, lost memory was no longer a problem. Whoever was trying to hurt me wouldn't have that added advantage anymore.

I spent time concentrating on memories about the Hispanic male who had invited me to have drinks on the night of the abduction. He said that he knew an old friend of mine who wanted to reconnect. It was going to be a surprise. While we waited for this friend to show up, I was offered a glass of wine. Soon after the drink, I started feeling out of it. The next thing I knew, I was in the Jeep and couldn't see the three men in the Jeep with me because my vision was blurred. The next thing I remembered was being upside down in the Jeep, and someone was on their hands and knees checking me. I was trying to talk, but he put his finger over his mouth as if to warn me to be quiet. Now I believed that person was Sam, and he had been sent to confirm that I was dead. He probably thought I was Kelly.

The bad news was that I couldn't remember where the house was where they had taken me either, except it was somewhere in the north valley of Albuquerque. It didn't help that I had never had a good sense of direction. So, I knew I wouldn't be able to find my way back there.

I then checked with Jim about what progress was being made with the investigation of the intruder who broke into my home and was still alive. Jim said that he wasn't talking, but both attackers were citizens of the US. The FBI had confirmed their ties to a Cartel, and they had felony backgrounds.

In Amarillo, though, there had been a major breakthrough. Capturing the offender who had dropped his cell phone was like hitting the lottery. It had a record of all the numbers called just before and after the estimated times of the murders. The offender had completely rolled over on everyone involved.

The team of investigators used him to capture a significant player connected to one of the Mexican cartels. They had a witness/informant motivated to cooperate, which was critical if they expected to make the necessary arrests.

Jane was in her second day after being wounded and was making progress but still on oxygen, was on a lot of pain medication, and not very lucid. She seemed to recognize her parents and me, but her speech was slurred. I was encouraged when she gripped my hand, though.

Katie met me at the hospital, and we sat next to her bed. Reverend Myers had visited and stayed for about an hour before returning to the Shelter. He led us in prayer for Jane's quick recovery before he left. Then he put his hand on my shoulder, "Are you okay?"

"I am for now but will be much better when Jane recovers. Then I will probably crash into a heap."

"She'll be okay."

Reverend Myers shook his head as he went out the door and said, "You all have been through an awful lot. Things are going to get better from here on out."

I just shrugged my shoulders and placed my palms together in a prayer position before thanking him for coming.

Katie said that Becky had tried to call her and had left a message that wasn't understandable. She seemed under a lot of stress because she was under an investigation that related to Sam.

After Jane's parents showed up for visiting at 5:00 pm, I left the hospital and returned to Jane's apartment. After eating an unhealthy meal of six doughnuts with coffee, I turned the TV on and started watching the local news. The news was very general about the crime at my house. The information from law enforcement was minimal.

I was relieved but worried at the same time. I couldn't keep my mind off of Jane, and I couldn't help wondering why we had gone through so much. In the past two months, I had been drugged, abducted, pushed off a cliff, suffered from amnesia, reunited with a girlfriend who had called me a selfish son of a bitch, and had killed an intruder who had broken into my home. And my girlfriend was shot in my house. If that wasn't enough, I learned about a lost twin brother that I had never gotten to meet and that a former friend had been murdered. It seemed as if it wasn't over yet either.

For the next couple of days, Jane made progress but was still hard to communicate with since she was drugged. I visited her each day, hoping we could speak and let her know that I was okay. But she was in and out of consciousness, so I wasn't sure she even knew who I was. Her prognosis was good, though. Reverend Myers advised me to take time off until Jane was better, and he visited her every day too.

On the fourth day, Jim telephoned me at 9:00 am and told me that he had some fantastic news and wanted to meet right away. I agreed to meet for coffee at Starbucks. But Jim said he wanted to stay in the parking lot to talk.

When I arrived in the Starbucks parking lot, I saw Jim's police unit parked as far away from the building as possible. I went through the drive-up window and bought a tall coffee with cream and sugar, another one with packets of sugar, and two containers of cream for Jim. I then parked next to the police unit and entered the unlocked passenger side door. After handing over the coffee, cream, and sugar, we shook hands. Jim then began to tell a tale that seemed incredible.

"Yesterday, the FBI geeks' discovered that calls were made from Jesus Maestas to two phone numbers just before the two murders in Amarillo. They confirmed a phone number was on the westside of Albuquerque. Jose said he had called a man named Gerald Espinosa. He told us that Gerald was the father of Becky Espinosa, who was dating Sam. He said that Gerald is connected with the Salona Cartel in Mexico. He created shell companies to help them launder money and profited from their drug business in the U.S. He, Juan Perez, at Juan's Plumbing, was one of Espinosa's main contacts in Albuquerque."

"Oh my God," I said as I looked down and shook my head.

Jim nodded. "But there is much more. The guy they caught in Amarillo who murdered Sam and his cousin agreed to let them record a phone call with Espinosa while using his cellphone. He contacted Espinosa and told Espinosa that he was in hiding and that he had followed Espinosa's orders to kill Sam and his cousin, but that things hadn't gone quite as planned. Espinosa lost his temper about contacting him at home but acknowledged the hit. By then, the FBI had already heard enough. When Jesus reached Juan, there was no answer. The FBI arrested Gerald Espinosa this morning but hadn't been able to find Juan. They think he has fled to Mexico."

"So, what does that mean for me?" I asked, sipping his coffee and eyeing Jim's facial expression.

"Well, for starters, I think you are much safer than Jesus," Jim smiled.

"Jesus will be under close protection while the trial is going on and then will do his time in the safest prison setting as possible. Gerald will be prosecuted by the federal courts and eventually end up incarcerated for some time, and his businesses will be ruined. The FBI is also investigating his daughter, Becky, for evidence tampering. We believe she was involved with some of the shell companies her father had set up to cloak the drug trafficking. The FBI will work closely with Mexico to find Juan."

"I guess I'll be involved in the trials too, right?" I asked.

"Of course, and your testimony will be important. It is unlikely that the guy who went after you in your home will confess but will certainly be convicted. He might eventually look for a deal since he knows he's going down," Jim sighed. "This case came together incredibly fast because everyone acted so quickly and with the help of amazing luck. As it turns out, the FBI and ATF had accomplished very little while monitoring Mr. Espinosa for some time, but this stuff fell right into their laps."

"Do you think Juan will come back to make another attempt on me?" I asked.

"Not him personally, but I think you'll need some protection until the trials are over. I think Juan's got a lot more pressing things to think about now. I'll keep you posted if I hear anything. Likewise, if you see anything unusual, please call me. But the ones who should be most worried are the rats leaving the ship."

I felt relieved and hopeful that anyone from the Cartel wouldn't figure it was worth coming after me. My testimony wasn't as critical as Gerald's and his connections.

Chapter 23

Reverend Myers, Jane's parents, Katie, Jim and I were in the hospital waiting room to visit Jane. She had been there for over a week and was showing real progress. She was even talking. The nurse invited us to come in, two at a time, to see her. The Dr. who was treating her said that Jane was fully conscious and communicating with medical staff.

I was excited to be able to talk with Jane and hear her voice. I also needed to feel her hand touching mine.

When we entered her room, Jane looked around the room and smiled. Her parents hugged her, and her mother held her for a couple of minutes. Her mother was wiping away tears during the entire exchange.

I waited until she looked at me and started towards her to hug and kiss her. Her eyes widened. She asked, "Who are you?"

I stepped back and gasped. "Not again," I thought.

The room fell silent for a moment before Jane tilted her head with a mischievous smile, and laughed, "Gotcha!"

I made an ugly face at her and then laughed, "That is so not funny!"

"Well... you said that one of the things you loved about me was how mischievous I was."

I just shook my head, hugged and kissed her all over her face.

Jim recounted the most recent events to the whole group and prepared us for what might happen in the future regarding the persons who caused this nightmare. He also gave a brief overview of how things would probably go on in court once all the offenders were arraigned. Gerald Espinosa was facing a litany of both federal and state charges and would likely get a life sentence. So far, it was proving hard to verify his daughter's actual participation in his illegal activities and the evidence showed that she might not have known as much about it as first thought. When her father was arrested though, she tried to get rid of some evidence to protect him, so she'll have to pay a price for that crime at least.

During the visit, I couldn't help but think about the lifetime friends I had made in the whole ordeal. I was content that something positive could come from terrible circumstances. I decided that I would eventually contact an aunt that I vaguely remembered, to see if she was still alive and might be able to shed any light on my family. For certain, there didn't seem to be very many relatives left but there had been a lot of secrets.

In retrospect, Sam had been a friend and I felt a sorry for him in spite of his behavior. He gambled his life away and that was sad. Worse, he had every advantage with his good looks, talents and abilities but had thrown them away. Regardless of his irresponsible conduct, Sam didn't deserve being murdered even though he had participated in the attempt on a life under duress. He had made some very bad choices and it made me realize that I hadn't really known him that well. He must have had some underlying problems in his life that pushed him the wrong way. Even sadder, his cousin was dead simply because he was Sam's relative and wanted to lend him a helping hand.

Jim reported that Mexican authorities were searching for Juan Perez and had agreed to work with the U.S. to capture him. If caught, he would be looking at extradition and a long sentence in a Federal prison. That was comforting and made me feel safer. Like many victims, I would monitor the incarceration of all of those involved so that I would know if or when they ever got out on parole or discharged. But... Juan had to be caught. So did the two men that got away in Amarillo.

My biggest gift was having my memory back and for the first time in a long time, a sense of direction.

I had doubted myself for years. After losing my memory, I had wondered if I was a decent human being and learned that I was. I also had found that I could be courageous when confronted with extreme fear. For the first time since I had lost my memory, I was confident about who I was and was experiencing optimism.

After all, I had been through, I was thrilled to have gotten another chance to be with Jane. Our journey was unique and worth fighting for.

I had gotten my life back. It was like a journey with all kinds of dangerous obstacles. It seemed like someone had stolen my life for a while, and getting it back was a beautiful gift. My very soul had been tested, but I was convinced now, more than ever, that good always conquers evil.